DUMMYLAND

DUMMYLAND

ACCOMPLICE 3

STEVE AYLETT

GOLLANCZ

LONDON

Copyright © Steve Aylett 2002

The right of Steve Aylett to be identified as the author
of this work has been asserted by him in accordance with
the Copyright, Designs and Patents Act 1988.

First published in Great Britain in 2002 by
Gollancz
An imprint of the Orion Publishing Group
Orion House, 5 Upper St Martin's Lane,
London WC2H 9EA

A CIP catalogue record for this book
is available, from the British Library

ISBN 0575 07087 0

Typeset by SetSystems Ltd,
Saffron Walden, Essex

Printed in Great Britain by
Clays Ltd, St Ives plc

hello Mum

Steve Aylett is author of *The Crime Studio*,
Bigot Hall, *Slaughtermatic*, *The Inflatable Volunteer*,
Toxicology, *Atom*, *Shamanspace*, *Only an Alligator*
and *The Velocity Gospel*

www.steveaylett.com

'Oh darling, we're really married.'
'And the dog makes three.'

—Bingo Violaine,
Intrigues of the Yellow Palace

Wahey, I'm dead. If I hadn't been so inept, the future could have had me. Sweeney, Emperor of Cold Hell, ate my entire brain and for ever after I was like a notion on parchment, fixed and useless, the philosopher Violaine everyone quoted to save them the work of thinking. Useless except that I had shouted something about a nemesis who could cause Sweeney a lot of problems. How did I know? The end of all things throws back a shadow. Barny Juno wound up as the focus for Sweeney's paranoia. Juno was almost a simpleton and often forgot about all this. If I were a whisper and not an atom trailed in ink, I'd tell him: this horizon's the merest posture of eternity. Stage blood, Barny. And he'd say he hadn't a clue what I was on about.

1

Viva Contraire

Immortality in heaven grows mundane

In the doll forge a dozen steaming mimiques stood rigid in a row. Behind them the express fiend machine was coughing sparks to the floor, its piston knuckles shuffling like a coinwalk trick. Lacquered eyes witnessed the head of rituals, the Grand Dollimo, entering via the gifts of a scaffold. He consulted a mechanical grimoire, a hinged mandala on its cover, and looked impassively down on the slurry-floored assembly area. He muttered, perusing the checklist. 'Brass springs under cardboard skin, eyes the same colour as the facial flesh, unguessable inner life. Good.' He called out. 'Accident faucets on.'

A burst of acrid metallic smoke flumed from the gauge wall, smogging the turbine hall and blasting past the hinge babies.

Near the end of the row, Maquette woke into the flavour of wooden teeth plugs and the rigid fit of her own jaw. She felt badly jointed, square-pegged into round holes. Her skin was crummy, barnacled with sprockets. The barbed wire veins in her wrists stung, sinuating.

Methylated monks drifted by. Before her she saw pipes and foundations, vents breathing each other's air. Large dark bugs trafficked the floorspace.

It was a simple and obvious matter to start running around, her clicking motions like surgery, and get out of this place which had given her only the aluminium winter of her head. Her little electric family was apparently dead. They didn't react as she skittered past rearing chuck jaws and mystery switches, out of the foundry and through the finishing shop in which she would never serve time. She was exploding through piled prosthetics and vestigial industralia before anyone could react.

Back on the observation platform, the Grand Dollimo was observing a number of floor lobsters with mangled legs and split shells, and a monk repeatedly counting the new frights and checking his sternum dial. The Dollimo strode to a window and watched a clattery imp with bracket ears scamper away from the process cathedral up Paid Preferential Treatment Street. 'Child,' he said, 'suffering is just another precision.'

There were no panes in the windows – the Dollimo wore a glass mask.

Finding a withered melon on the front step, Gregor gloomily considered his lifestyle. Five glad bugs on a bedspread, one disconsolate whimper and a head which was no particular shape – these were the spoils of a string of damaging episodes, the last of which had involved his molesting a civic monument. In his sub-basement bedroom irrigation pumps chilled his dreams and there wasn't enough room for time to pass. And he arose to find this kind of scornful relic, left stealthily in the early hours. Once he had stumbled upon a burnt pork chop which seemed to resemble his own face. A note which accompanied a tusked skull, reading 'Letters: where are they?' had seemed blotched with tears and led Gregor to suspect it all related to some service badly done – but beyond this he was confounded. He had wrapped the flaky head in newspaper and given it to a child in the town square. The note he had thrown in the furnace with all the other baffling trash which arrived unceasingly at the sorting office.

Though he lived below the office he no longer worked

there – his shot nerves and mallow shoulders now bore the weight of Deluge Trousers, Reticent Greeting Cards, Preburnt Diaries and Deadly Carpet Samples. The latter, impregnated with lethal effluvia and venom, was a steady seller for Stampede Door to Door Products.

Keg-shaped and plodding, he bumped into Edgy on the way out. Edgy was a stringy guy with a head like a cinder chimney. Today he turned up for work in a tropical shirt, Bermuda shorts and jelly sandals. He looked up at the ripe sky. 'Ah what a beautiful day to offer you the opportunity of a lifetime Round One. What's in the sample case?'

Gregor felt he was on a patch of rare sure ground. 'A couple of new winners, as a matter of fact. The Table Chaffinch – a chaffinch which stands on the table and is otherwise unprepared to do anything. The Damaged Radiator, exactly what it sounds like. The Levity Closet, that's doing well. The Doggone Diagram, this big technical poster here – see? There's circles round the equation there. That shape in the corner I don't know what that means.'

Edgy scrutinised the baffling blueprint. 'This all you got, my friend?' He sounded concerned.

'What about this? It's a sort of jellied slug but it's got a first class mind, maybe. Because I can, I make you a present of it.'

'This is a coin, Round One. It's so long since you took one out it's shrivelled up like a navel.'

'Really? Well there's this collapsed husk I just found, I guess I could sell that. Yeah I could clean the grit off and call it Worse Than You. Whatever happens, you can compare yourself with this and say, "Well, at least I don't look like that thing." They will when they're dead and rotted, but by then they will have paid up and I'll . . . why you looking at me like that?'

'Round One, this isn't a dried husk – not the way you mean. This is a drylord seed, a dormant judge. You've got to take this to a legal guy and pay for the hatching. Scratchy scribe with innards like an insect. Nostrils too close together and feelings learnt from a book. It must be about that display during the Mayor's speech.'

Gregor felt weak. 'I'm going to court? Well ... what happens?'

'Each viper takes a turn to give their own unsettling rendition of the facts. I saw it – now who else?'

'Everyone in the town.'

'That's right, I remember now – everyone. We were all stood there laughing at the Mayor and then you appeared with a funny look on your face, humping one of those statues on the town clock.'

'Don't keep explaining it to me, I know how it was.'

'In fact now that I think about it, it's just about undeniable. This spore guy's probably the only fella who wasn't there that day. But that's the beauty of these drylords, Round One – they don't have a clue what's going on in the world until they hear it in the courtroom.'

'Well, if someone can be charmed by a beanbag, I'm in with a chance.'

'Has anyone ever been charmed by a beanbag?'

'I bet they have. Certainly they have. With the beanbags they're making these days? It's a lock.'

'You're damned, Round One.'

'I know.'

'What have they done to you Round One. Look at you. You're lurching from one fulfilling success to another. Carry on like this you'll be selling one welly near the subway. Laying with only the midday traffic for company. Nothing learnt and new shrugs like the old from our friend Bubba here. Hey, Boo – a strange iridescent sheen on your face there, what's happening?'

Barny had wandered slowly through the heatwashed morning towards the sorting office, looking at a fun book about animals. He still didn't know that by annoying the king o' demons a while back he was the motivating force for every recent atrocity in the town. Barny passed tough reptilian plants, callboxes raw as a baboon's ass – local calls only –

and jettisoned shells of transport. The few traffic lights in Accomplice changed with the seasons, beginning green in summer, then through yellow to a lovely russet red in the autumn when, like fallen leaves, they could be ignored. 'I'm in love,' he replied.

'How d'you know?'

'I haven't got any money.'

'That's why you're so thoughtful?'

'I've been tending to a woolly monkey. He was crying and I hugged him for a long time. Oh, and I brought you a book.'

Edgy browsed about in the proferred book which was called *Coping with Leopards*, with the subtitle 'It's the Most You Can Hope For'. He read aloud. ' "If I've learnt one thing, it's that animals don't like going backwards. But they will approve of it in you – even stalk toward you with a snarly expression to encourage it. Yes sir, one rule for the powerful, another for us." And a quote from Violaine at the front – "Fiction is not a threat to those who know the difference." Thanks, Bubba.'

'There's a small section on panthers,' added Barny as Edgy tucked the volume away.

'Well, Gregor here's had the grey pineapple and expects to pay for the proceedings by selling Deluge Trousers and other crap that's going begging in the marketplace. Gregor, you're planting your arse on scanty soil. Think you can create a buzz on an old product, like Hootry the fruitman? You know what he did? He started referring to the fruit as "marooned bladders", without transition or warning. Within nine days his entire market base had dried up – nobody wanted what he had to sell. And here I am offering a golden chance.'

'I haven't heard any golden chance from you,' Gregor spat, and slap-folded the Doggone Diagram in preparation to leave.

Barny piped up. 'If you need money, Gregor, why not get it from Fang, *he's* a bag man.'

'He's a *bog* man,' Edgy corrected him. 'And maybe he'll join my scheme if you two won't.'

'Oh, the beach bar idea?'

'No, that's a long-term dream. But I could finance it with my notion to obtain the illegal meat of the Quadraface harpies – they live in the swamp, you eat the meat, you go invisible, you can do whatever you want, everyone'll want to buy the stuff. A reindeer doesn't know that does it?'

Gregor pushed the poster into his bag. 'That's your justification for everything isn't it, Plantin? A reindeer.'

'I've never seen a reindeer,' said Barny thoughtfully and smiled, chuffed by his imaginings. 'But I'd love to. They're the only deer where males, females and calves produce antlers. They shed their antlers annually.'

'Manually?'

'Annually, Edgy. Then new antler growth in the spring and summer is nourished by a vascular covering called velvet.'

'Antlers,' Edgy mused dreamily. 'Now that's living.'

'I don't mind going to the swamp tonight, Edgy. I'm not sleeping.'

'Monkeys again, Bubba?'

'No, I keep having a terrible dream. But I've got to go to the swamp to visit the barbers. Crash Test Nureyev told me the barber knew all there is to know about bats – I may be able to get one to replace the bat I accidentally sent to heaven the other day. It's a special kind, otherwise I'd just use one of the ones we snog at the office. You ever go to the barber's, Edgy?'

'That would be admitting there's a problem. Anyway I've been scheming for weeks to get this harpy meat deal sorted – any expedition has to be planned in fly-leg detail. Glad to hear you're in, Round One.'

'I never said I was in,' Gregor blurted aghast, but Barny had begun describing his dream, immersing one and all in the involuntary imaginings of a man whose philosophy was less complex than a Swiss roll.

In the dream, he was with his girlfriend Chloe Low, sitting on a rock over see-through water. The bay was as still as a mirror. They could see the Announcement Horse posing half a mile away. Then EH Hunt appeared, a rather ominous-looking huge fellow dragging a treasure chest over the cauli-flower rocks. 'What's in the chest, EH Hunt?' Chloe asked.

'Perhaps a complicated jasperflower, who knows?' he smiled, winking.

'Is it?'

'Well, no,' muttered Hunt, and as always when embarrassed, he began frantically pointing out the wonders of the deep. 'Mermaid chow,' he said, 'and ours too.' Barny and Chloe looked at tinkling shrimp of thin glass, seahorses like corners of toast, a studfish pullulating across the seafloor like an ulcer and a marine mouth which moved by blurting sandy water. 'Hey Barny, that's so funny,' said Chloe, and pointed out an underwater man, scar incarnate, its head a white scream, surfacing fast at them.

Barny stood quickly and found himself near the Church of Automata in easy conversation with the shaman Beltane Carom. 'Like I told your friend, there's a day between Thursday and Friday which the angels use,' said Beltane, who was now the trickster Prancer Diego. As in many dreams, the two people had become mixed together. 'Someone keeps slipping through. But that's another story.'

'Whatever this is, it's getting old.' In the dream Barny was thinking about flies and humans, and how being everywhere was not the same as having conquered.

'The truth doesn't get old, Juniper. And I don't hear you suggesting anything better. Except that stupid thing about spinning dogs.'

Nearby, workmen were pouring the foundation for a new Gubba Man. Every year a few psychologically vulnerable diggers were swallowed by ectoplasmic white holes while their colleagues laughed unharmed. Accomplice was a sun-trap lidding an etheric mesh of connecting tunnels, the creepchannel. This toxic tissue formed a subterranean transit system for demons on the way to people's breakdowns.

'I don't know what you're talking about. I just want to

care for the winged and stepping animals of the earth, and be happy.'

'When Sweeney's killer surfaces, you will have another sadness. Motive is another person's reason. Live on mere motive, and what makes one thing visible will hide another.' Then the figure whispered in a different voice again, 'I won't be here forever. I go on the record for the day you work it out.'

Barny looked away down the street. Some sort of shabby replica of a child ran up to shrill his face and Barny bolted awake in his hammock, staring about at the joists and rigging of Ladderland, his ramshackle home. Windows painted moss-green, honeysuckle flourishing out of the floor and the lion asleep on the second deck.

The dream was in fact a pretty good prophecy of the mayhem programmed for later in the form of Rakeman, who was even now approaching Accomplice in search of a horizontal mirror to exit shrieking. This tumbleweed skeleton wasn't modally boned and so proceeded to the upper world almost like a worm, shuffling through unspent geology against the flow of lawyers coming the other way. One of these lawyers was Max Gaffer. Undamned but brash, he saw opportunities below and chugged downward in a scarcar he had stolen from Mike Abblatia at the gas station. The car was hardwired for tragedy, six dozen auric plug arrays birthing servitors under the hood. Its silver grey bodywork was corroding with the vomit transmission fluids of the creepchannel. Already Gaffer felt at home. Here the lies were like rain repeatedly overcoming the steady work of the windshield wipers.

He was navigating a mesh of connecting tunnels, yellow bile speedways flurrying with a million popcorn skulls, all sick and aglow. Migraine patterns rotted the windows, spinal fluid bursting into the cab and turning the car into a sudden eruption of bugs. Gaffer swallowed hell. Lost, he was decanted from an ectoplasmic portal in the ceiling of Sweeney's cavern and landed through an expensive glass coffee table.

Stumbling awkward, he looked up at the titanic mantis which bent almost double to view him from above. Scallop-backed and armatured, its every movement made a ratcheting echo in the freaked cavern. Coaxial spite veins spread from its thorax to the chamber walls. The elongated skull, which was the size of a family car, opened out at the front like a Swiss Army knife. 'You have an ulterior nervous system,' it rumbled. 'A lawyer, am I right?'

Gaffer stepped unsteadily out of the useless table frame. 'Max Gaffer, your Majesty. Distortion's the game – I pretend it's not a luxury, or that there's such a superabundance of truth that the luxury of distortion is okay for a laugh.' He brushed the glass powder from his ruined suit, straightening his cuffs.

'Gaffer. When you contacted me through that piece of rotten meat I wasn't sure whether to see you. It's not particularly convenient.'

'Well, as the philosopher Bingo Violaine said, "Voyage ignorant, arrive surprised."'

'You begin badly, lawyer. That ambitious patsy died at my jaws. It was him prophesied that Barny Juno would be my nemesis – just to gall me in the interim. His removed looks are barely remembered except for those stupid sayings.'

'My sentiments exactly, Majesty – and as a shadow of my sincerity, I've brought this chilled piece of brass, hammered into the general shape of a huge maggot.' Gaffer held the offering aloft into the yellow air pain of ghost sickness.

'Put it on your head,' Sweeney commanded.

Gaffer missed a beat. 'Of course,' he said with a frown, and balanced the metal maggot carefully upon his head.

The infernal grandee leaned back a little, coaxial nerve cables swaying around him. 'Speak.'

'Well, your Majesty, as you rightly guessed, I specialise in the hobbling of humanity.'

'Humanity? I call it "prattle meat".'

'The hobbling of prattle meat.' Gaffer gave a colourless laugh. 'I pretend to conceal a large sentiment behind my licence, but in fact there's only a piece of plywood and then the wall. See how false and polished I am. Unbeatable. The condition of forgiveness is always makeshift, and temporary – I do better. In fact I swindle away and Accomplice sits like a plaster pig.'

'Yes, that's all very well but you're really nothing to me. The way things are at the moment, henchmen and cronies are two a penny. In any case I've got a plan in hand already with a classic shrike demon I've sent above.'

'Special pleading, your majesty. I work for the Mayor. He's had trouble with the simpleton Barny Juno, who I know has raised your clattering hackles in the past. I can manoeuvre the situation however you like up there, as an inside agent. In fact, a strange blob-like friend of Juno's is being taken to court and I'll be prosecuting, all according to the law. Juno will be called as a witness, his blank face and shapeless keks a shame on the town. I shall incriminate him before a judge made mostly of air.'

'Thousands of these barbed nerves work the law.' Sweeney twanged the nerve net with an auxiliary mandible. 'Your efforts are mine already.'

'The targeting is all,' Gaffer stated with due deference. 'And opportunity. The law is a collection of intimidations which stands for nothing at ground level – but within the court it poses as reality. No truth. All there is hell and negotiable.'

'Hell on earth, I know,' said Sweeney wearily, sitting back in thought. 'That *was* the idea, after all. Physics and fate being what they are, one place is as good as another.'

On closer examination the shell at Sweeney's back was a giant leathery chair, holding him in with fanned measures of gut. Gaffer was feeling sick with the effluvial air and raw, cold electricity. He had to wrap up the pitch. 'So what's the point in succeeding solemnly?'

'You think I've lost sight of the ideal? Allowed Juno to weary me?'

Gaffer just let it ride.

'Allow me to limit you with congratulations,' the demon announced suddenly. 'I do happen to have a vacancy at present. The demon Feroce will show you to your quarters. Oh, first you'll have to eat this.'

An arm like a white branch anglepoised toward him, the claw at its end holding something like a black starfish the size of an angel cake. Gaffer took the crusty thing tentatively – it was as light and dry as a biscuit. 'Is that really all there is to it?' he asked. As he put it in his mouth he glimpsed the blowhole gupping at the star's centre.

'Just a core creature.'

Gaffer's throat was slit vertically all the way to his chest as the core creature went down, a vivid heart blooming on his starched shirt. Blood vapour clouded from his mouth. The brass maggot crashed from his head. He tore at his clothes, exposing his chest as the creature shot its barbs and anchored there, the blowhole showing like a third nipple. A bony grey blade cuckooed from the hole.

'Alright?' Sweeney chirped.

A large upright dog of skin trotted over to Gaffer and began to pull him away by the arm, not letting go when the screaming lawyer fell to writhing convulsions in the frost. Dragging him, it looked ahead with eyes like the navel of an orange. 'Don't touch the underwear,' Gaffer choked, strangely comforted by the sheer mundanity of the request.

Maquette had skirted the centre of town but enough people had seen her by nightfall to give everyone the heebie-jeebies. Some shouted 'What?' and others went 'Ah!' in a high frequency. She had overturned some trash behind Snorters cafe only because it seemed the thing to do. People were in there working their munching units.

Some people seemed woolly. Some were more colourful than others. One of them danced around.

She passed around the back of what was obviously a school for chefs – there was steam and mayhem in there, and an evil more tangible than any she had encountered thus far. A group of chefs gathered amid the polished steel, the master chef presiding. 'A stringy bird'll convert them for a while, but we need something that accords with our principles. We have trapped night for years in a portable cabinet. Their mouths at last rely upon our meals. It's time for the final phase. Not yet but soon, and then there'll be no more real food.'

She hurried on, ball-joints clicking, shapes tumbling past her. Twists of car and cacti to a calmer district. She was looking up at a green onion-domed building. In the silence she heard her own head.

2

The Pool of Tears

Templates can't stand a masterpiece

Barny entered the swamp in the dead of night, clinging to the roof of a strange concrete train which screamed from nowhere to nowhere – most people entered the swamp this way, leaping to safety before the ghostly machine swerved out of existence. Though he lived to care for the winged and stepping animals of the earth, Barny had killed both with one stone when he inadvertently caused the death of his parents' pet bat. Edgy advised him to visit Crash Test Nureyev for advice. Nureyev was the main man at Feeble Champ Books. 'Interested in furry winged pigs are you?'

'Bats,' said Barny.

'Indeed, well, I never published anything about bats. Want to hear the good news? The idea was poison to me because I associate those flapping monsters with the barber.'

There was only one barber in Accomplice. 'Out in the swamp?'

'Yes, he's got about a thousand clasped on his roof so densely they look like layered lead. I became attuned to their squeal frequency during a particularly harrowing visit.'

Crash Test Nureyev had once gone to the barber wanting a beard, and the barber nodded, agreeing silently to sit with him for the duration. They sat unmoving for forty-three days. Finally the barber roused himself, gesturing Nureyev to the chair.

'A pointed beard demands discipline from the wearer – are you equal to it?'

Had the barber asked forty-three days earlier, Nureyev would have chuffed a laugh of scorn. Yet now, haggard and starving, riven with insects, jumpy with irregular sleep, he was no longer certain of anything. Staggering into the swamp, he floated blank-faced down a waterway until it emptied hot into the sea. When he was washed up on the shore the Announcement Horse declared him an unprecedented gobshite.

Barny picked past trees twisted like chewed candy and pondscum rich as mustard, stopping amid the nervy Rizla crackle of dragonflies. The barber's porch was lit with a spiral lantern. The roof hung from a horizon of sausage blood and indeed a thousand bats lay upon it like composting leaves. Barny entered the shack. Like many swamp structures, the walls were fused with onion glue. In one corner was an earthenware statue of an electric fan and on the back wall a poster saying 'Tired of your abilities? Join the army.' There was a protocol to be followed in this tiny place.

'Why venture you into a quagmire writhing with predators?' asked the barber, a tall man in a false moustache and deceased suit.

'Because I dared to dream of a haircut.'

'This extraordinary admission makes us brothers. Sit you down.'

Barny faced the mirror, next to which a framed sign read: 'You pay me to oppose your preferences.'

'Would you keep it down to a low roar, sir?' the barber insisted suddenly, and began by knocking the round hand mirror to the floor. It was against his code to acknowledge the mistake immediately, and as he danced attendance upon Barny's head, he did not see the demon Rakeman twisting up toward this perfect doorway.

Time passed, the barber making small moves and large, and releasing an occasonal cry. The meagre lights sometimes guttered. Barny's face floated in the wall mirror like a cartoon moon. A watersnake entered, showed some interest, then flexed out again, leaving a helix diagram in the sawdust. The barber made a few folksy remarks. 'Anyone applying make-up in quiet grief, sir, I raise my glass.'

'Yes.'

White as a tap root, Rakeman ascended toward the etheric porthole, the knurls of its spine spiralling around its body like a screw threat.

'Monks certainly are silent, sir.'

'Yes, they are.'

The barber pulled at a few head corners, his expressions shockingly arbitrary. 'Your good father, sir, was fishing nearby – I happened to notice he has the manner of hairstyle which would cause cattle to stampede.' Barny's father had a sort of huge, glowing octopus of hair which Barny had given him for his birthday. The barber apparently didn't like the idea of trying to tackle it.

'He has.'

'I think we're all done.'

Rakeman was an instant from entry when the barber plucked the mirror up and tipped the demon back into icy space.

'Dozens of nights will replace each other before it returns to its former glory,' the barber remarked, angling the mirror around Barny's oblivious head. 'Anything else?'

Having climbed the roof, stolen a small Mariana fruit-bat from the throng and slid screaming into the swamp, Barny departed the barber's neighbourhood with the man's professional curses ringing in his ears, such as 'May your love fumble in the lock' and 'Doves will attack.' Both curses would be effective – but when the doves attacked days later, Barny would be suffering a terrible cold, and with nothing on which to blow his nose he considered the sudden white flurry a gift from heaven, snorting into them and casting them aside.

*

Maquette explored the domed observatory, looking at charts of spiderwebbed skies. The tall round windows were transparent clocks pinned with a glass hour and minute hand. The whole place was inset with such technical emblems. And in a chamber at the middle of the building, she ran in on an old man in a cane armchair, who turned rotten yellow eyes upon her. She was turning to leave when he called out, 'Don't rush past me. Disobey my mouth and be devastated by the dog.' The old man indicated a cat which was relaxing nearby. 'Come here, let me grab your face.'

Maquette approached uncertainly, and the old man reached out, running his hands over her features. The cat shook its tail, producing a sound like a rattlesnake.

'So it's like that is it?' said the astronomer. 'Eyebrows like pinball paddles, a sort of teflon snout and a hinged flap for a mouth. Well, the last's not so unusual. Must you see a person's argument before you see through it? Yes, if there's truly something there. So I never needed my eyes much. Sit you down, child – and don't mind the dog, his bark's worse than his bite.'

The doll sat on the hard floor and looked directly up at the lenticular roof.

'I do without window certainty, of course,' said the old man. 'Got some fella with a strange sort of head who helps me out here with the observations – Getty. A good assistant's rare – they just come apart in your hands really. But I see plenty. Pictures swell into my head like filling sails. Amino acid in a vase, get your imagination in there and stir. That's the golden concentration. I could drive this chair forever.' He crushed himself in a little more. 'This whole place, bricks no bigger than a sixpence. A real home has life in its walls. And I don't just mean the rats and so on. The open air means something different. Winter exchanges flowers for heavy breathing – does it advance the relationship? Nature is obstinate by moving around. Think on that, if you can with that artificial arrangement of yours. Clouds are the blunt end of infinity. Myself I shoot dead wood down the cash slot but it's not enough. Gaps grow together and we've got a meaning – call that culture? Their values even exist, if in a ghostly form. Ah, good years sink to the bottom of my memory.' He gave two sighs – or maybe he was breathing. Maquette had removed her eyes and was toying with the idea of offering them to him. One rolled towards the cat, who was instantly alert. Maquette quickly retrieved it, stuffing both eyes back into her face.

'I used to put the colours among the putty, I tell you,' the old man was saying. '"Toad for a shilling mister." Ho ho! Picture the scene, me panting in connection with a cab-horse. Disaster you might think, but at a penny a shot my invitations were accepted. Know what I told him? Back to the grave with you and your twelve and six! My legs, of course, were smashed. Well, a cup of tea builds character in an asylum, if thrown at the right moment.'

'Thank you, sir,' said Maquette, standing.

'Off already? What, ashamed of your piping?' He called after her as she walked through some curving stone corridors. She found another room, which seemed to be a device library. Reaching on tiptoe to beckon an object from one of the shelves she caught a movement in the side of her eye – something angled outside the window. She got behind the door and peered in. The demon seemed to perch on creaking air, then clamped to the window frame and tucked its wings away, ducking into the room. It stepped down and was immediately examining a timepiece and strolling about. Its head was silver and its body was folded white vinyl.

A shadow spread down from a corner and across the floor toward the silver thing. It became dense and roiled up, a dark, armoured demon with a head like an industrial vice. Maquette retreated sharply, scuttling away.

The demon Dietrich Hammerwire clipped past striping dimensional edits, occasionally sampling the flavours of a passing bandwidth. A bunch of bright green squares and blue warmth caught him and sucked him down as though through the nostrils of a plughole. He tided out into the local reality, firming up.

The blade-silver Gettysburg, a demon with a head like a spike-mine, turned his platinum eyes on the new arrival.

'I heard you'd finally defected from Sweeney's repetitive realm. How are you feeling?'

'A bit gassy.'

'Well, for the moment you're pasted on this reality like a leaf on the surface of a pond. Your few possessions are hell surplus. It'll be strange for a while.'

'You know me as being of iron control,' Dietrich said.

Getty seemed amused. 'Oh I know exactly how it is – why you're here. Your reserves of evil were maxed-out. A chance of something. Honesty and conclusions, clean as nature. Anyone who studies nature knows that murder is superfluous. I speeded history once, then looked away – saw a blur of billions coming down the pike in escape from the rules.'

'Even the slightest end has impact.'

Getty was acting over-casual about this encounter. The bookshelves were racked with wallclocks, slotting in sideways – he would occasionally slide one out and turn its face forward, browsing the time, each one different. 'You think so? You don't know this world.'

'So this is your understanding of my actions is it?' Dietrich's scarred wings were hunching like shoulders. 'While in fact, what's attempted below is here perfected. Humanity can begin a season in the abstract and end it with blood in the roads. The day does not contain one hour of time that makes sense. A barcode baby falls out of the cake and no one thinks to scream. That's the sort of thing we're dealing with. Their behaviour is chaotic. Their distortions are undirected and crude. Their rebellion against authority is no rebellion at all.'

'They see no reason to dismiss something which they never recognised in the first place. You and me, we're interbeings, smelling always of bonfire. Half the time I go undisguised, not just here caring for the blind man. We're a couple of exotics having a chat amid the mundane, so what?'

'Liberated are they? You think it's only the geology that keeps these people here? The canyon, the sea? They can't think out. EH Hunt and that shaman are the only ones who've been elsewhere and who believes them? That's why it's such an occasion when the circus comes to town.'

'And that's true too.' Getty stared at him openly. 'So regret me.'

Part of Dietrich seemed to concede – he relaxed a little, watching a random distance which was drawn across the window. 'Well, how do you suggest I occupy myself?'

Gettysburg considered. 'Discover twenty sentiments in an oak, whittling. Watch stories zigzag through town. Lobby gringo sells narcotics and knuckly root crops hulk in miniature. Remember the rest with alcoholics and you're laughing.'

'Hobbies?' Dietrich said with scorn. He turned from the window, the sky impressed on his face.

'Maybe.'

Dietrich was beginning to see how the new hell operated. This place worked like a jigsaw. Nothing would be a whole pain again.

Barny pushed through a thicket of grandmothers and approached his parents' shack, entering through a side window. The canary cage which had housed the fruit-bat was empty – only a sad fragment of apple lay on the papered floor. He handed the new bat into the cage and walked quietly out to the porch. His father was sat there on a rocking chair, the massive cilia of his hair phosphorescing the area. 'Well, look what the bat dragged in,' said the old man. He stated in no more than five words what he hoped for Barny in the future, and Barny asked after his health. 'Oh I shan't complain – though I've been married for years, I'm determined to remain optimistic no matter what. You're still seeing Chloe Low?'

'Yes, father.'

'Long legs are short term. And don't call me that. As Violaine said, "Things are as bad as our short time alive will allow." And the eclipse is coming.'

'I was telling the leopard about that.'

'The leopard. Listens does he.'

'Well, yes. While doing other things.'

'Like what.'

'Well, pouncing. Chewing, you know, that sort of thing.'

'Chewing,' said Pa Juno with thin contempt. 'I remember the last eclipse – your mother stopped talking a while. And there was a hell of a storm. Birds were liquidized in the air.'

'I would have screamed.'

'So would I but there wasn't time. A friend of mine, Tommy Franks, started going bonkers in the head. Threatened him but he thought I was joking. No imagination, that one. So the future's a blank for him anyway, why should he care if I conk him on the face a few times with a timber? That was my reasoning at the time. Before I could act, a moose came a-bellowing out of the forest, rammed him with its antlers and ploughed him through a load-bearing wall. That brought him down a peg or two. The headstone said: "Here lies Tommy Franks, acquainted with death but never previously to this extent." But look, all explanations are hopeless.'

'It wasn't a reindeer?'

'Reindeer? In my whole life I haven't seen a single one. Your mother thought so too. I told her five times – which was a lot in those days – "That was no reindeer." I'm a little tired of hearing about it.' And he started coughing.

Barny was about to reveal the kind act which he hoped would compensate for the bat incident and the perhaps forgotten matter of the alligator, when Pa Juno piped up again. 'I bet the Mayor'll use the eclipse as another excuse to spend money on himself – money they could have spent on mending the flyover and clearing the sloths off of there.

Even the stones are rotten, it's a crying shame. What do you do to help the community, boy?'

'I won the Deadly Snake Contest with my viper Misses Kennedy,' Barny told him proudly. 'I was up against Tamale Wired For Sound and Tony Fleet's Rubber Hose.'

Pa Juno stared at him, momentarily speechless.

'I suppose you know there are no more vases in the whole of Accomplice because of you and that snake of yours? Get rid of the reptile or I'll take it by the tail and crack it like a whip so as its head flies off into the grass. Hey, Ethel,' he called, 'do you hear what your son's about now?'

At that moment Barny's mother emerged from the shack, limping with grief. She was wailing 'Dead and eaten by a furry winged pig' and then weeping 'Our brittle friend is gone' or something like that, and Pa Juno stood to get the facts from her. It seemed that Barny's replacement bat had eaten Lovely Ramone, an exotic katydid which had the camouflage ability to resemble a fragment of apple. The pet bug had been a balm to their previous grief and now Barny had inflicted yet another unprovoked cruelty upon the household. 'Your son belongs in a p-p-paddock,' his mother sobbed, mortified.

Pa Juno held fast to his wife, glaring in affronted ferment at the whey-faced and retreating Barny. 'Get away from here, disaster boy – back to that menagerie of yours. Back to your hill station! You're no son of mine!'

Fondling one of his auxiliary chins, Mayor Rudloe poised on a wooden horse for a portrait. *This moment would be fun if twenty kingdoms were mine*, he thought. He was trying to look proud but didn't really know anything about it. Max Gaffer had recommended Undo Cakewalk as a fine painter – Undo in fact was known to have emulsioned the walls of a couple of sheds and was meant to be painting GI Bill's house right now, so not only was he due to disappoint the Mayor but to get smashed to the floor by GI Bill. The portrait thus far resembled that of a charred thermostat smothered in onions. Mayor Rudloe was giving the man the standard speech he reserved for employees. 'If you were more emotionally intelligent you'd have better tools to pretend you want to be here and I, as the fella who explained this to you, would be embedded from the get-go as a benign authority—' Max Gaffer entered the office. 'What is it, Max?'

Gaffer was uncomfortable, his bones still howling with cold electricity, the yellowed frost of hell crusted on his guts. There was grit in the collars of his eye-sockets. He moved in a chemical pain. He was confounded that normality could feel exactly like this, a devil's hand in your pocket.

'Well, what is it? Speak up man! You been beaten up again?' The Mayor broke his stance, frowning at Gaffer's bloody shirt.

Gaffer halted startled an instant at Cakewalk's canvas, then pulled himself together.

'Eh? Oh that's it exactly sir, no fooling you – by a gang of screaming children, their gills venting scarlet. Said gills were everything, and tried to cut me some with a fast knife.'

'Those bastards. One day the technology will be in place to understand what they're on about. Pack up for now, boy,' he waved dismissively at the painter, 'my head'll be roughly the same shape when you return.'

Cakewalk dragged the canvas stand through floor lobsters scattered here and there like smashed telephones, and closed the door behind him.

'We need to discuss the matter of public celebration around the eclipse, sir.'

'Celebration – bah!' The Mayor slowly dismounted, stepping directly onto a carapace which burst with a loud report. 'Oh yes they show the bit when everyone throws their hats in the air but not the mumbling, scuffing business of sorting ownership afterwards.'

Gaffer handed him a folder. 'I've been drawing up guidelines on exactly how much strutting is acceptable.'

'The fuseheads won't like it,' said the Mayor, sitting down

24

to examine the document. 'They've got that ritual, the strutting procedures.'

'Well there's always some special interest group, isn't there.'

'It says here "I take up the pewter sword of the blag". What's that about? And why organise a special event? What's the racket in an embrace? I get repeated and ringing endorsements for my reign of terror. My unassailable office allows me to speak modestly. The distribution of cooperative morons is consistent across the district. Acquiescence is faster than we can handle these days. I think you'll find democracy is more than enough for servants.'

'Unbeatable, sir. But you're forgetting that certainty, along with a mansion, is a signal to the general herd that your right to life doesn't apply.'

'You mean they'll hate me and then kill?'

'They may do both simultaneously. Right process wrong smile, these matters are delicate. And in cases of emergency, our robbing of the citizenry cannot be held up by the matter of their consent. Better to pre-empt such bloody violence.'

'They had a roaring good time with the rioters' pageant.'

'Pageant? That was a *riot*, sir.'

'Yes. So what must I secrete in the midst of these people to make them respond any more?'

'Well, there's a simple way to get a million feet beating their way to your face.'

'Of course – millipedes, a whole sack of 'em! Max, you're a genius.'

Gaffer coughed politely. 'A festival of Accomplice culture, sir. Music, drama, like that, by and for the people. Hold it in the Scar Garden, surrounded by statues of the populace. It'll point up the bland as positive, waste people's energy and soften the tone. Sentiment is ignorant of history. And nothing lasts longer than the effects of unkindness. Time some conventional revelations for next year and you're laughing, lit from below.'

'You mordantly cynical young hound,' chuckled the

Mayor thoughtfully. 'How did a monster like you come to be in the world?'

'By the time I was aware of anything the whole affair had been arranged.'

'That's grand. Well, a cultural fair. Buffoons and the stink of failure. Bastards farther than the eye can see. And to the finest exhibitor I'll award a bound edition of my collected speeches.'

As speech-giver, raconteur and sudden bellower from windows the Mayor's oeuvre contained a good many classics including 'I Serve You Though You Sicken Me', 'Look at the State of You', 'This Sea of Gawking Faces' and the more mature, resigned tone of 'I Realise I'm Stranded Here'. Among policy speeches were 'I Will Destroy All Other Candidates', 'Burn, You Mother' and the hardline 'I Will Make It More Expensive', as well as the sympathy bid 'I Kick Snails Away But They Keep on Coming' during which Rudloe collapsed into quiet tears. 'Hello, Mate' and 'You Will Become Dust' played well both in their separate forms and as the combination barnstormer 'Hello, Mate. You Will Become Dust.' Other philosophical and contemplative monologues were 'Bang – Sorrow!', 'Am I Really So Chubby?' and 'My Thirteen Thousand Misgivings', an epic diatribe about everyone he remembered seeing or meeting. His personal favourites were the boastful 'Trousers Won't Contain It', the pugnacious 'Yes, This Is My Eleventh Corned Beef Sandwich', the truculent 'Lurk Here, Lurk There, You Champion Bastards' and the knockabout nonsense of 'Arly Barley Fell Me Where I Stand'. He even displayed some humour in the safety talks 'Head – Don't Travel Without One!' and 'Thank God For Chainmail', and the left cheek of his arse in 'Get a Load of This'.

'The other matter concerns a trial in which I'm taking part. That spud-like thing who had sex with a statue during your "You Want a Piece of Me?" speech – a friend of Barny Juno. Of course, you'll want me to completely absolve Juno of any complicity during the case.'

'Eh, what's this? Who?'

'Barny Juno who is of course always beyond reproach.'

'Juno? Beyond? Damn it isn't this the same bastard who held a funeral for a lizard and dropped his trousers during the eulogy?'

'That's him.'

'Didn't think twice about coming in here dressed as an ape. Released a croc in a crowded theatre. Threw a death-adder in the air during my "You Aimless Wonders" speech.'

'Had eight hundred eels in his garden,' Gaffer added, looking thoughtful and reluctant – he was carefully and visibly conceding to the Mayor's view. 'And it was a grizzly he dressed as, when he came in here.'

'Dressed as an ape in here and rode a lion into the shelter, wrecking our attempt to sell these poison insects to the poor as food.' And the Mayor kicked at one of the huge carpet bugs, merely snapping an antenna like an asparagus spear. 'He's probably in charge of that wooden midget everyone's seeing.'

'Wooden midget?'

'Where the hell have you been, Max? There's a toddling mechanical doll putting the frighteners on one and all. It clicked its rigid head against the window at Snorters cafe apparently.'

'Of course,' said Gaffer, thinking instantly of the Church of Automata. 'Yes, it's got Juno written all over it.'

'Really? Then the trial's the perfect opportunity to have Juno executed as an intolerable nuisance. As Bingo Violaine said, "Activity is often wastefully over-wrought – for instance, only one small lesson can be learnt from an avalanche."'

'Outstanding, sir,' Gaffer nodded, and on the floor around him a number of blurs appeared like lens-faults, drying into intricate glass. The forms filled out to solid black and red, ratcheting their many legs. A dozen new floor lobsters had swelled to life, the visible ticks of corruption.

3

Chapterhouse

Any good insolence accommodates whole universes

Conspicuous and powerless, he had stood on a ledge apparently for fun. He maybe deserved all this walking and walking through the town on the way to a grim appointment with a preserved man. Veering aside into the cakeworks, Gregor was halted by the proprietor.

'Door admission amigo,' said the man sadly. He had a drooping beard where his moustache should have been.

'Adds up to nothing,' Gregor improvised nervously, and the man gestured to the bounty of his store. Gregor selected a large morgan cake. 'I could spend a lot of time eating this.'

The baker wrapped the merchandise. 'Enjoy it, señor.'

'I'm looking forward to it already.'

'I wish I was in your place, señor, and young.'

Gregor left the store. That night the baker would write in his journal: *I was indifferent as to whether he should survive the encounter. There were certain decorations on the cake. If he failed to see the beauty in this arrangement, that is his problem unto eternity.*

Gregor trolled on, holding in one hand the bagged cake and in the other a grey husk the size of a pineapple – the drylord seed. As he entered the offices of De'ath & Destruction, ancient automated needles plunged into his arms, halting him in pain and drawing fluids from his body. It was like a red levy extraction except that the fluid seemed to be water, not blood. The needles retracted into the doorframe and he proceeded, feeling dry and dead tired.

'You're a great man for the statues I hear,' said a beetle-like man rattling in the trouble of his cases. Worn-out citations on the gloomwall were the only bit of flash in this twilight world of legal stationery. Even the floor lobsters were sluggish and enervated, some mere husks. 'I've been selected to witness your blistering defeat at trial.'

'Aren't you defending me?'

'Of course – I was using legal terminology. De'ath's the name. That's the seed is it.' De'ath took the drylord seed from Gregor and carried it with a sort of brisk reverence to a pale wooden cabinet which resembled an upright coffin. Opening this, he placed the papery spore on an upper shelf. He closed the door and turned back to Gregor. 'Well now – what else have you got there? Oh dear, I can't evaluate a cake like this. Either eat it all now or put it in the floor cupboard over there, out of my sight.' As Gregor did so, De'ath sat on the edge of a desk, one of the 'normal fella techniques' he had learnt at desiccation college, and glanced at a file. 'The courthouse is grown from boneseed, as you know, and has to be grown anew for each new case. The cornerstone is formed by a piece of thigh-bone removed from the innocent party. You'll have to go see a surgeon – here's a note for Dr Perfect, you know him?'

'He's the one who told me I was some sort of walking potato.'

'That's the one – he's got an entirely visible brain. Don't mention it to him, he's sensitive about the old noggin. In the past fiends have sprung from his study, breaking through heavy crates and tumbling furiously into a pond. Unexpected even for a famous cynic. These are the fluids we removed at our front door, by the way, already sealed in plastic, you see?' The lawyer tossed the laminated block into the bin.

'How long will the court take to grow?'

'Eight months, a year, two years.'

'I can't wait two years for justice.'

De'ath went into a fit of hacking laughter. 'You'll wait forever for that, Round One. But the court may take a couple of years. It all starts with the principle that the facts of the case can be discovered only by the utmost severity, and so this severity will instead be directed toward you yourself. Expect an ambush of embarrassments and urgent disgust. Your fiasco of a face won't help.'

'According to Edgy my face is shaped like a cloud.'

'Exactly, so people see whatever they want in it – and in this case it'll be horror and perversion.' De'ath carked with laughter, his left cheek ripping to release a spuff of colourless dust.

BB Henrietta, a strong blonde whose head resembled an exploded sack of flour, worked in the sorting office with Edgy. When she heard about Barny's weird dream, she began telling one and all it was balls-out obvious she should base a play on it for the Miasma of Culture the Mayor had announced. BB was the one for amateur dramatics and had last year put on a thing called *Standing Brick in Hand, Rain* in which lank worms were blown at the audience out of a tennis server while GI Bill lumpenly recited the Violaine monologue which began: 'The ashes of my club may choke you, baffling the battle record' and ended with the words 'You are *super-wrong!*' being repeated fifty times.

BB Henrietta itemised her new plan in Snorters cafe and when Edgy's girlfriend Amy Gort declared herself in to write the project, Edgy began juddering violently and holding onto a stranger's face for support. Amy's last written effort had gone like this:

troubled protocol,
rain and wet,
field botanists screaming,
'I am slung over a branch.'

He was determined, this time, to prevent it. 'Amy,' he said raggedly. 'Darling? Leave it out. My little chicksands? Leave it out, I . . .'

A caterwauling interrupted his efforts, echoing through the streets outside, and he found he could protest no more.

It was some days before the facts were established. The trickster Prancer Diego had caused bloody havoc in the Square by releasing a parrot directly into a gran's face. The traumatised old woman had run amok, climbing a tower and hurling years of stored abuse upon the town. Condensed and purified over time, her scorn was so meticulous it had caused everyone alive to black out for forty minutes.

In the observatory the artificial child Maquette returned to the central chamber to find the old astronomer slumped aside in his chair, and the cat simply laying nearby. In fright and confusion she ran from the domed building. Everything was silent but for the wind and the distant hiss of the sea. She toddled down the lane and through a gate into a small field of redgrass and parked cows. Beyond this was an area of rusted greens and planted heads which eyed her silently as she passed. A man in a woollen hat was sitting against the wall of a brown shed and Maquette stood looking at him until he woke up and squinted at her.

As for the old gran, she was left on the tower ledge to desiccate, remaining there like the shuffled husk of an insect. To point out the corpse would have been to remind one and all of the shameful incident, so it was ignored even when it rustled in the breeze.

'When a cold glass child steams completed in the slamming powerhouse, we give our creation the respect it deserves,' stated the Grand Dollimo. Wearing a monochrome suit, city bowler and glass mask, he faced Gaffer across the mechanical desk. 'Since Celadon, the first doll struck in our forges, was a mere statuette in a fiery womb, we have corresponded cosmic to the trouble engineer. The mannequinade are a stillborn sisterhood and all the scarier for it.' His eyes moved behind the mask like those of a reptile behind its nictitating membrane.

Gaffer wasn't about to argue – the Dollimo had given him a short tour of the process cathedral, pointing out junk tracks and scaffolding. Dolls dragged around like cockroaches as the masked man rifled through skull drawers, removing punnets of cracked glass eyes and implements in scratched and studded steel. 'This artefact hand is for collectors only. The new dolls leave the mouth out of the loop, their hearts scream direct. Look at this torso, full of hairpins, stale rubberbands and seventies dust. This one's got a vocabulary – from fiction. And this head's built round an old human skull.'

'It's a bit flaky,' Gaffer had ventured.

'An experiment. Cross the transfusion factory here, watch your step – this is as busy as the algorithm deanery gets but the monks' work is vital.'

All had a patina of iron dust and dead perfume. And now in the office, Gaffer was hard-put to gather his pitch. 'I finally surpass the dead in social satisfaction. What a delightful tour. Carbon scoring everywhere. And, er . . . I share your concern with your little latch-knee kid.'

'Maquette. An empty force child – clock logic keeps her aglow, mayhem in her lobes.' The Dollimo seemed to be attempting a dismissive tone to render the content utterly banal. 'Yes, her brain is a calamity manufactured using oxygen-free copper.'

'Indeed?' Gaffer forced a meaningless smile. 'Well, over at Rudloe Manor . . . the Mayor shouldn't be losing sleep over a toy-sized fright. No one should, but the Mayor, there's the Miasma of Culture to organise, and so on . . .'

'The Mayor is not our concern.'

'Mayor Rudloe is corrupt so you don't have to be.'

'In that, Mayor Rudloe is presumptuous.'

'Should we have reason to doubt your loyalty?'

The Dollimo's expression shifted like a fish in murky water. 'I've no reason to care.'

'Be that as it may, there's a theory that your church presents a robotic front to avoid the red levy. Bloodless and thus nothing to give.'

'Our position is a matter of record, Mr Gaffer. No regrets and a soldered coffin. What is a mask when nothing is behind it?'

'The Cannonites—'

'The Powderhouse is a mere crybaby temple, their inordinate revelry an evasion. A break in our church is every loser's dream.'

Gaffer gestured to a NO ENTRY door which led from the office. 'You have secrets. Maybe this doll knows a few. In any case we can't have distorted tin children running about the place. Now, in the Mayor's office we see this as an opportunity for a two-for-one. We've reason to believe your escapee is intending to liaise with Barny Juno, a notorious mooncalf.'

'Why.'

'Juno lives to care for the winged and stepping animals of the earth. The girl's full of gears and he wishes to protect her. What could be more natural? We could pool our resources in the pesky chore of snaring this cocky little replica, while silencing Juno into the bargain.'

'We have no argument with this simpleton Juno.'

'Oh, a stranger's just an enemy you haven't made yet. No one would pretend you were strangling anything other than a deserving bastard. Deny the doll's your work. I could see it wasn't brought in by anyone else, by giving the job to the Brigade.'

'If there's any strangling to be done, it'll be done by this gentleman,' stated the Dollimo. He pressed a copper button on the desk and the whole deal jawed open like a trash compactor. A weird sentry elevated out of the mechanism and stepped aside, the teeth of the door clicked shut. This thing was a man of red wax, its head seamed like a football. 'Distaff Plastique, my lethal chaperone and bloodshed assistant.'

'Out . . . outstanding,' Gaffer gargled.

'Distaff's only got one ingredient. He's skin stretched over a pulse.'

Gaffer looked at Distaff's vinyl face. The mask paid no attention to him.

'Now,' said the Grand Dollimo, 'we influence the dead hand of the voter. And you? Lost in admiration for the brilliance of your own underwear, you might forget every promise you ever made.'

'Me? I distribute the situation to benefit all.'

The Grand Dollimo shunted open a drawer and removed a riveted metal mask. He smacked it down on the desk. 'This is the Iron Smile. It forces the wearer's face into a smile no matter how unhappy he is. It is screwed directly into the face, through skin and into the skullwall.'

'A threat?'

'A bargain.'

Putting pills on string for re-use like a teabag, Doctor Perfect sensed his patients, a dry death rattle beyond his door. He went to look – an endomorphic idiot was sat in the time lounge, stumped by a kiddie puzzle. 'The square hole shouldn't be that intriguing, laddie.'

Gregor looked up without comprehension. He was feeling worn, having inherited the hyperactive Magenta Blaze from Barny. She had credited him with seduction and he was disconsolate. She even let it slide when he told her about nap chickens, the squabbling fowl he thought he heard when on the edge of sleep or snoozing fitfully in the daytime. He had decided to set up a camera to get the phenomenon on film. And now here was the Doctor with his exposed brain and all. It was a man's world alright.

The Doctor's bare skull tackle was grubbier than ever,

rinds of dirty fat hanging off like ravellings from a hat, and the flies were a busy cloud.

The surgery was situated underground and cool rootwater fell from the ceiling, pulping documents and staining furniture. Gregor upset a tray of organ forks as he followed Perfect inside. 'That's right, larva boy,' Perfect muttered. 'Wreck my life. I've been inquiring after the printed gouge records since they told me. "Riding a public monument" wasn't it? I heard all about it – who didn't, after all? This insanity of yours is a model of its kind. Anyway, legal cornerstones are a rare treat for me. Some say the prosecution of victimless crimes like yours leaves the structure weak. We'll see, won't we?'

Gregor looked at the smashed anatomy angel on the back wall and the two crushed cars which served as dissecting tables. 'What's that?' asked Gregor, pointing to the object on the second vehicle. It looked like a mess of exploded lard.

'I've been dissecting a Gubba Man.'

Gregor gibbered – Gubba Men were statue-like figures which dotted the town and which grabbed you if you went to them for help. Once grabbed it was almost impossible to disentangle yourself from these officially-appointed sentinels – starvation and lack of progress would follow.

'Have a look, while I prepare. Glance through this surgical lens, it'll make it worse. Illness stylised, that's the aim.'

Gregor looked through the dish-like magnifying glass – it was like looking into a dish of milk.

'It's something like solid scar tissue,' said Doctor Perfect as he pulled on some bloody scrubs. 'Or cheesed milk.' He looked over Gregor's shoulder. 'Ah, the heart, king of veins. Notice the total lack of characteristics. I name the more crucial flesh and damn the rest for wasting my time. In a sense this is the perfect control subject. Anyway, laddie, it's time for your surgery. A few people organise a set of spare bones for this sort of thing – you haven't thought that far ahead I suppose?'

'I don't have any,' thought Gregor. 'Why didn't I think of spare bones? What a dope!'

'Alright, get up on the car. A lazy muscle is a watery muscle. It's annoying and probably illegal. There you go. It's good that you're wearing those stupid shorts, less work for me. Watch the nerve screen up there. Let me see . . . Operation 40, I think.'

Gregor lay back on the thundery roof and stared up at a suspended glass bowl which was veined like an eye. He tried making conversation. 'Ever met Karloff Velocet, Doc? Got a problem similar to yours.'

'Problem?'

'But worse – it's all stuffed in his hat.'

'I have no problem, except when an occasional experiment goes wrong.'

'How can it go wrong, if it's an experiment?'

'Be quiet now. I'm making the incision and flaying bare your upper leg.'

On the screen, skin opened like a rose. Gregor was shot through with a chemical pain.

'Screaming in a patient is to be expected,' said Doctor Perfect. 'Surgery done gingerly is mere infatuation.'

Gregor stopped shrieking long enough to see bones amid the blood like drowned architecture.

'Red-and-white-nuggets, red-and-white-nuggets, what to do? Eeeny-meeny-miny-mo. I'll just scrape the cartilage out of there – you don't need that.'

'Are you . . . sure?' asked Gregor. His leg was coming unglued.

'I open the people but death claims their innards.' Doctor Perfect scraped away as though buttering toast. 'The extraction's a simple matter of torque. I . . .' Perfect levelled a heavy wrench into the wound.

Gregor woke up on a wooden bench, a thermometer in his mouth. He sat up and found a plastic bowl on the floor. In it was something like a big lump of slimy china. He looked at his leg. There was no bandage – it seemed to have already healed over. The Doctor appeared. 'What happened to the hole?' Gregor asked him.

'I plugged it with Gubba Man stuff,' said the Doctor. 'Just an experiment. Saves having to embroider the patients.'

Gregor took the thermometer from his mouth. It depicted a scarlet skeleton.

4

Blood from a Stone

Long accidents rub your face in it

Barny was with his girlfriend Chloe Low, sitting on a rock over see-through water. The bay was as still as a mirror. They could see the Announcement Horse posing half a mile away. Barny looked down at seahorses like corners of toast and a studfish pullulating across the seafloor like an ulcer.

Chloe turned to him, her short black hair flicking a bit in the breeze. 'BB Henrietta told me about this play of hers – I don't like the idea of our lives being splashed all over the stage, Barny.'

'It's not about us – it's a dream I had. We were sitting next to the sea and something leapt out at us. Then I talked to the shaman about it.'

'Did I ever tell you about Ong Jahbulon?' Chloe said. Every week she told Barny a story connected with stuff in her father's curio museum – she spent her time trailing about through those catacombs, poring over stored storms, Zeto lights and ampules of combustible moth dust. There were severed doors in the basement, died and dried like picked skin. And now that she had someone to tell, it had become a fierce habit. 'There's a diary of his dreams in the Juice Museum. Everything he dreamed came true, and he was horrified by the objective results of his nightmares. He became resolved to stay awake, and set out to find stuff that would hold his interest. But society being what it is, the most recent interesting event was the appearance of a giant hernia in the local aqueduct, as a result of one of his dreams.'

Barny's eyes followed a marine mouth which moved by blurting sandy water – then spotted something like a starved white tree floating toward the surface.

'So Jahbulon allowed himself an occasional dream to give him something interesting enough to keep awake. But when he did dream, it was always about the real results of his dreams – and so the dreams became inbred. Can you guess what happened next?'

Barny realised the thing was an underwater man, scar incarnate, its head a white scream, surfacing fast at them. He was just beginning to holler when the mirrored surface of the water exploded in white sparks, the spectral man shattering as a small fish flew out and over their heads. Behind them, EH Hunt reeled in the capering creature, laughing fit to burst. 'Finally a shorthump of rest, eh, fishy? Golden seafood, I love it. Eels are eels but so what, bite the head off. There's seabass out there, and eleven dolphins. Seaweed too, the entrails of the sea.' He was already cooking it, spinning it on a spit so fast it blurred. 'The narwhal has no dorsal fin,' he shouted, bellowing with hilarity.

'Fish aren't edible, Mr Hunt,' said Barny.

'Can't I, boy?' Hunt took the fish and bit into it. *'Can't I?'*

Chloe calmed Barny as they wandered toward the town. 'He's right, Barny – the chefs don't like to admit it, but pasta hasn't always been the staple diet for humans. In fact, did I ever tell you about Widey Dantooey? There's a calcium picture of him in the Juice Museum. He studied fish and discovered they make themselves the same density as their surroundings by means of a swim bladder. So he ate hundreds of swim bladders, hoping that he'd be able to hover through the air. But he only made himself the same density as water, and when the chefs tried to drown him—'

'What the hell's that?' Barny asked as they passed the Ultimatum Restaurant – he was pointing at Gregor, who was walking along with a nugget of bloody bone.

'From my leg. I'm going to the courthouse lot, want to come?' asked Gregor dismally. They followed him to the grey hardpan of the courthouse lot. Nothing grew here but the courthouse – not even pale weeds. It was a little deliberate desert. All three of them began to feel heavy and oppressed. Gregor pushed the chunk of bone into a cement sinkhole in the north-east corner. 'Let's get out of here. I want to see what state my statue's in after that operation.'

'Did I ever tell you about Korova Laddfrith?' said Chloe, feeling antsy and backed up. She had to finish a story. They crossed the square, dodging herds of flappy swine as she told them about it. 'There's a blueprint baby of his in the Juice Museum. You know everyone in Accomplice has a statue in Scardummy Garden. Even animals and demons. And if anyone dies, their statue crumbles and disappears. But there was one time when someone died but still had a statue in the Garden. Laddfrith was a rust artist who was always enraged by the critics' inability to understand that his iron sculptures changed and improved with age. He finally constructed a strange sculpture in the Garden and invited the dullest critic to see it, intending to kill him on arrival. He could have smashed the critic's statue, but the principle of statucide would have meant he himself would also die.'

The three entered the white and green statue garden. Here stones were born hot in the weeds and grew amid panama crows and eastergrass. Many of the statues were decked with clothes and decoration, some topped with soft hats. Gregor's, when they found it, more than anything resembled a giant spud. Its real-life double gazed upon it with a thoughtful expression. Apparently no item of his own body was too commonplace to consume Gregor's interest.

'The rust sculpture was a sort of frame scorpion,' Chloe continued, 'and since this creature had been built on site and cemented into the soil of the Garden, it took form in the community and immediately scampered to find Laddfrith. The sculptor tried to fend it off with a mixer of industrial cement. When the critic showed up, he saw Laddfrith holding the mixer over his head and being set upon by the iron scorpion, tipping the cement over himself. A few minutes later, Laddfrith's statue crumbled. But the cement had hardened on the real Laddfrith and, to this day . . .'

Gregor suddenly leapt onto his statue and started humping up and down like there was no tomorrow.

'Wha . . .?' Chloe had put up with a lot since stepping out with Barny, nearly every day being pecked by an adder or socked in the nose by a chimp. On one occasion a duckbilled platypus had slapped her senseless with his tail. But this potato man, abusing himself as no one had ever self-abused before while staring glazedly into the middle distance? 'Barny, it's bad enough that you're ignoring me in favour of the winged and stepping animals of the earth but these friends of yours? Look at Gregor. Why's he doing all this?'

At that moment Edgy loped into the Garden, looking for Gregor, and smirked to see the Round One's antics. 'I see Gregor's almost weightless, nettlesome brain is running wild. Who says there are no more heroes, eh?'

'You see?' Chloe continued urgently. 'Edgy's head, that exploded cheroot again? He's probably having a good laugh about it now.'

'He's right here,' said Barny, 'he's not laughing.'

'Oh I don't know what I'm saying, out of the way—' And she got all choked up, storming off.

Gregor finally seemed to decide that he had done all that was required of him, and dazedly dismounted.

They stood in amber sunlight, not looking at each other for a while. A vine was growing against a south-facing bastard. A bug like a belt buckle stop-started across the flagstones.

'She was right about your head, Edgy.'

'My face is stringy, I'm a boy.'

'Feast your perishable eyes,' said Sweeney, viewing the scene as reflected in the bloodshot deeps of the Ruby Aspict. 'It's starting to work. Rakeman's influence, even in nightmare.

That's how demons used to work – spoke into blood to influence. Juno's powers are fracturing.'

Max Gaffer stood in the chill voltage, shifts in dread evaporating and reforming as the king corpuscle slowly turned. 'Why not just pound a coffin together and get rid of the bastard. I spoke to the Dollimo, a head of one of the church cartels – he's charged some sort of automatic man to deal with all the wearisome business of murder.'

'We'll be more thorough than that – Rakeman'll bring him down here, through the nearest mirror. Its head's all ring muscle, you see.'

'I don't quite believe in the child-man Barny Juno being formidable in any way.'

'Of course you don't. He wears bewilderment as others might wear armour. You've come quite late to this caper. Seeing matters from both of two opposing sides can be limiting in ways you may not appreciate. Your predecessor, Dietrich Hammerwire, yay high, anvil for a head – he took me for all I was worth and then defected above. Why? To bother only one direction at a time? To eat the biscuits available up there?' The thought seemed to occupy the ivory demon too fully for him to continue. The chitin scaffold of his body towered against glaring phosphorus. 'Anyway it's madness to do the same thing over and over and expect a different result.'

'Unless you account for changes in external circumstances.'

'Shut up – get out of here. And don't upset the flesh valence in your chest – it'll want out. How is it, by the way?'

'It hurts like a cast-iron bitch, to be frank.'

'Good, good. Off you go.'

Edgy and Gregor walked down Ken Blurn's a Coper Street. 'I've got everything we need for the swamp expedition, Round One. Are you aware again of what's going on around you? Hear what I'm saying? I went to the Shop of a Thousand Spiders and covered every eventuality, including your bloody death. I got a spirit knife of white glass, a benthic brace, a bottle of bone, a cathay claw, a cornercage, an october switch for making visible what is invisible and four betsy lamps for attracting ghosts and irreversible trouble. Those harpies won't know what hit 'em. As Violaine said, "Yield to doubt and glimpse a world of possibilities." Anyway I paid the goat and nearly got out of there before that Spooky Staring Boy said anything, but he collared me at the door.'

'What did the boy say?' asked Gregor raggedly.

' "Black eggs in the sleeper." '

'What did you get in case of my bloody death?'

'Raisins.'

'Huh.'

'So it's on for tonight – we're catching the ether express.'

5

The Man with the Vegetable Head

Voters play with the moment

'Sorry I couldn't see you earlier Mr Lucent – I was balls-deep in work.' King Verbal stood briskly from behind his desk and strode to shake the chef's hand – he led Quandia Lucent to a plush seat and returned happily to his own, backlit by a delicate fishbone window. 'Yes, I've seen you at the Ultimatum Restaurant and wanted to chat with you a while – we have the same philosophy, I believe.' He indicated an ornamental bone fireplace which flared to the ceiling, the company motto pressed into its polished face: 'Garbage at crippling prices.'

'We cut convoluted meat into merchandise,' the chef conceded.

'Your candour does you credit.' He inspected Lucent with easy curiosity. 'You run the chef school too, don't you?'

'I teach others how to take a chicken and cuff off its head.'

'Cuff? You mean "cut" off its head.'

'I know what I mean.'

'Well, what can I do for you Mr Lucent?'

'You probably know we take our orders from an overgrown seahorse in a cupboard, which lives on a diet of desiccat packets from appliance packaging.'

'I'd heard as much, as rumour.'

'I'm happy to confirm it – within these walls.'

'I understand.'

'We are aiming for one hundred per cent pasta consumption within two years. In truth, we're almost there. Customers exist to serve us, as you know. They can't get enough of whatever's placed before them. They order salad, we give them pasta, we call it "pasta salad", they don't even blink.'

'And what a boon to you. Pasta's instant, complete trash and costs nothing to produce.'

'Exactly. People are feeble, powerless. A waiter is an authority figure by the mere fact of bringing their dessert.'

'This explains why waiters are occasionally burnt in the Square.'

'Indeed – I was right about you, Mr Verbal.'

'Oh, I've been there – cheap supply? When I first tested boneseed, the initial seeding was done in a graveyard – many of the houses I grew had the stretched skulls of our ancestors doing a visual scream out of the walls. Crazy days. Wild. Later on, dispersal was accomplished by a berserking pig with a couple of saddle bags. Never too soon for that sort of mayhem.'

'You anticipate my major point: cheap resources. The work of the Boneseed Company has interested us for some time. Architects: they lattice parliament, barbwire the train, sense the box most like a building and use that as a basis. The human race succeeded in dim light, in bitter cold – why not in a world made of pasta? Steaming keeps and cathedrals of pasta, lax doors, slick walls, sweating vistas of slimy impermanence. Join with us and you will want for no resource.'

King Verbal regarded him with cagey good humour. 'I like you, Lucent, we're on the same page with this corporate crime malarky. Monopolies are just so flagrant they're delicious.'

'Then you will consider it.'

'I'll think damn hard about it.'

'This is as much as I can ask. Good day.'

When the chef had gone, Verbal skinned a cigar and lit up, frowning happily. It had always seemed to him that the scattershot petulance of chefs was designed to distract from their shame at having evolved with no natural enemies. But this guy Lucent lived calm in a plan. Pasta towns? Verbal stared into trancey smoke.

An hour later he was on the phone to the centrifuge coven when his next appointment was ushered in – he cheerfully gestured Max Gaffer to sit down, completed his call and gave the lawyer his happy attention. 'That was the lab, they borrowed seven tons of salt from the decency commission and it's pure flour, riven with slugs. Useless for our purposes – and for theirs too, wouldn't you have thought?'

'I couldn't possibly comment,' Gaffer smiled.

Verbal chuckled. 'You sly young dog. To what do I owe the pleasure? Another wing on that cranial pad of yours, you ergomaniac? Baby teeth pushing from walls, something new for the ladies. Or how about this – mashed glass, a beautiful new concept in windows. You can tell your old windows it's been real but—'

'I'm afraid this is a more . . . delicate matter.'

'Oh?'

'A certain criminal got a cornerstone order a short time ago – you've probably received a request to regrow the court.'

'Indeed we have, just yesterday.'

'The Mayor would like you to expedite matters. This criminal is an associate of Barny Juno, who as you know, has killed and killed again.'

'I heard he threw an apple core at the Mayor.'

'It's true,' Gaffer muttered regretfully, 'that he came into the office eating an apple and threw the chog at our leader. Lobbed it underarm so it defined an arc and gave everyone time to think on the inevitability of things.'

'But hardly murder.'

'The point is, the Mayor has charged me to bring down this social nuisance one way or another. I've been given carte blanche really, to withhold certain words, barge in a bit, ignore various matters, whatever I like.'

'Of course, my cooperation will be full and hearty – insect

paste maybe, that could speed development, but lifespan also . . . When do you want the courthouse complete?'

'Three days.'

Verbal whistled. 'Well, there may be a way but disintegration might accelerate too – in fact the structure could become necrotic almost immediately.'

'Appropriate isn't it, for a court? See what you can do – good.' Gaffer stood to leave. 'I know I can rely on you.'

Alone again, Verbal sat in thought a while, then plucked up the phone and got the lab on the line. 'Fletch? Don't throw the flour away. Put water in the vats. We're trying something new.'

Maquette liked it out here in the growlands. Here were car wrecks cooking red in the greengage field, finger posts rotted to tobacco-coloured powder and miles of bushes tangled with brown windblown audiotape, trailing down to the sea. The bobble-hatted Kenny Reactor told her of nights he spent gazing at the familiar living necklace of plant lights. 'Over there are globe roses, the glasshouse is mainly sports gear hydroponics, in that corner are drylord specials, and here are my heads. All my heads are legal, there's no blood in them. Look.' He dragged a head from the soil, its hairy tuber root trailing along. Taking up a half-moon knife, he sliced the thick matter in half, showing Maquette the cross-section. He indicated the packed outer leaves. 'These tight, hard cabbagey layers are the mind imitation called "chadder". These look like spore arrays but they're actually chemical fuses. This centre starshape is the code heart of any grexian planthead like this. These are the lock fluids, which filter through to the ruff of valve sprouts around the neck. The plasma is flushed down these channels and collected for use in blond beer. All this tangled grey fibre is about water drawing, like any plant.' He turned the lobe, the glitter of moisture moving in the sun. 'This is the face.' He pushed some of the rooty hair aside. There was a fungal, expressionless human face, brimming amid itself. It was almost blank, its eyes like coins. Its lips were yellow blebs like the ears of cacti.

Maquette heard a crunching from beyond the hedge and ran into the shed, cotter pins ticking. Next door was a small allotment of fire alarms, red as tomatoes – their owner had wandered over to banter with Kenny on the matter of apple butter and lemonics. 'If you're such a country boy, Reactor, what does it mean when the cows lie down?'

'That they've been killed for food.'

'I mean the other time.'

As their talk continued, Maquette picked up a dirty mirror and propped it on the seed table. Wedging a trowel into the seam which passed down the right side of her head, she prised at the crack. When the face tilted open, she could see a dark organisation inside. Her glass eyes were set amid some dusty grey valves, antique wire, frozen gears and a gummed-up gasometer display. The door of her teeth clicked shut.

Kenny Reactor came in and stopped, holding a seed tray full of bonce eggs. 'Hiding out, eh? Burying something here is dangerous.' He put down the tray and looked at her open face. Then he closed it for her. 'Maybe some animal hair,' he suggested, 'and some colour.'

Barny had been so distracted by the nightmares and all, he had missed the main event. Every moment of Chloe's body was like liquid gold. Now Barny felt like there were tiny lights drifting into his mouth, blotting out. He was making the world dark. He never thought to go argue with her – Barny assumed that everyone meant what they said and did.

Shuttering up in the ramped and cabined landscape of his house, he lay his head on the lion. 'Oh, Mister Braintree,' he said. 'I wish I had a beak. A colourful one.' The lion yawned and slopped his mouth closed. He slowly whipped his tail – it was like a golden rope tipped with a fluffy teardrop.

Chimps eager to play instead found themselves hugged in silence.

Barny finally dragged over to see his friend and auxiliary father-figure Mr Peterson, who sat poolside wearing Jonathan glasses and considering the glass in his glass right hand. 'I'm in your debt after that bit of driving you did for me, Bubba. If it's a matter of money, just say the word.'

'No, Mr Peterson, it's Chloe. I could climb her like a tree. But my scary nightmares have made her go away.'

'Old John Satan with his eighty nostrils and his horns the shape of question marks eh? If you don't have at least ten demons prodding at your eyes round here you've got some explaining to do apparently. See that butterfly over there on the hedge? That flippy thing's more worthy of respect than you.'

'Why, Mr Peterson?'

'Because *it's* an adult. *It's* due to die any time. It's a question of perspective.'

'Is that the question? I dunno . . .'

'When you're chortling, you think you know a secret. Then you forget the secret, you forget you ever chortled, you make a sandwich. Yuh get older and mirrors choke your smile. Keep drinking railroad paint, Bubba, and cherish each little mood. If they mended that flyover you could go see the world. Wind of the high roads, straight and disappearing. But as it is, these escapades of yours . . . To a man like me they're just baffling and that's all.'

'Me too, Mr Peterson. I don't ask for it. Any of it.'

'Well, I'm scheduled to shrug my shoulders and punch the wardrobe at six. Get outta here.'

Barny decided to go and see the shaman Beltane Carom in his strange garden. A slogan over the arched doorway said: 'A tree is not in doubt.' This was of no help at all. He entered the flowered and fountained pattern yard. The flooring was concentrated into a dense oracle schematic which was of no interest to Barny. Beltane Carom sat in the mosaic centre playing a board game of arcane components. Barny explained about the demon nightmares and Chloe. 'I'm scared.'

'Hell is the fifth season. It operates behind the other four.

Look.' Beltane pointed to the air and there appeared a sharp second of vast reality. 'It's the spatial mating of this realm and theirs.'

'What do I do, Mr Carom?'

'There's a defector demon living over at the observatory – I'll give him a call.' Beltane took down a mirror from the ivied garden wall and placed it flat on the ground. 'This is a spiral induction,' he said, and repeated a few obscurities. The silver demon Gettysburg folded up via subspace with shivery wings. He listened to the shaman's account of Barny's problem, and in response suggested that Barny confront the monster in his dream.

'Lamp the bastard with whatever's lying around,' said Gettysburg. 'Then you'll wake up, like that.'

'Thank you ma'am,' said Barny, oblivious to the demon's affront. And he left, feeling a little better.

Gettysburg stayed on a while in the yard, chatting to the shaman. 'Eyebrows in the back of his head, that one.'

'He's not a fool, just preoccupied, is all,' said the shaman. 'It's somehow put him at an axis point for anyone or anything that goes berserk. Like a catalyst, he himself is barely affected. I think *The Eleventeen* calls it a rumble hub. I once saw Barny in the Square. He was crying loads and looking at a picture of a collie. The dog had wet eyes and he explained the animal had died four years ago.'

The notion brought forth a dog from the air, a mere protein brow, semi-formed, which evaporated.

'I think I recognise the demon he described from his dream,' said Gettysburg. 'It's Rakeman, a real vintage fright. The eclipse might help it through. Sweeney too, for that matter.'

'It's like chess, isn't it? Each piece of the story is deep and goes right to the middle. Something's made Accomplice mathematical. Someone with a plan. You can feel it can't you?'

'The doll?'

'I don't think so. Probably the lawyer.'

'Dietrich mentioned that lawyer had sent a rot message to Sweeney.'

'Dietrich,' Beltane muttered. 'What is it with you two?'

'Typical interbeings, I'd say. Like everything, trying to grow. Even that doll's trying in its way.'

'Yes, I screened her progress from the observatory to the hydroponics ground. No one was conscious. As Violaine said, "If a memo burns faster than you can read it, nature is telling you something."'

6

Psychodelta

The slots of a pig's nose are precise enough

Flashlights flitted through brackish smoke in the deep tree night. Gregor always struggled when called upon to stray from his role as a sweating, door-to-door dupe. Covered in marsh flukes, rollmaps and packs, he ducked under the keening of honey buzzards and called ahead to Edgy. 'This place is really crummy. What are these – tree pogs? "Water Tupelo". What's the point? These plants are completely uneven. They don't know what the hell they're doing.'

'We're in a swamp, Round One, a swamp. At least the slime stops them from being creaky, eh?'

'This is the crappiest line of approach we could have used out here.'

'This line of approach is an absolute peach and you know it. We'll find the wise woman Feral Beryl, ask her how to catch them glass harpies and bam's your uncle. There's nothing she doesn't know about harpies, or anything, any subject. She's a top-flight wise woman with a face you could use for a can opener.'

The mashy ground logged their energy and stained their pants. Fogs were slowly drugging a swollen landscape of wrecked foundry graves and casks of false blood dried solid. Here was an old truck sunk to the waist, mossed as furry as a caterpillar.

'For instance, at what point did you become a part of this

landscape? It depends on someone else's viewpoint doesn't it? Well, the harpies play with that. Their four-sided heads disengage their image from your perceptions by going one or more better.'

Gregor's senses were getting shredded by the endless disarray of jungle gloom, the lurching heavy sky and untuned colours. 'This is taking ages,' he said.

'Hey, you know that thing you did with your statue,' said Edgy. 'It was really gay.'

'What do you expect? I've got Gubba Man stuff in my leg – I'm part cop now.'

'Quiet – there she is.'

She sat amid a sparse scattering of white piano bones on a plum-coloured hill, stirring a bucket of bee venom. Her face was whorled and flaky as bark.

They were starting up the slope when the crone cried out. 'What the hell are you doing?'

'Why not?'

'I didn't ask why, what the hell's that thing?' She pointed at Gregor.

'Human detritus,' said Edgy, and winked at Gregor.

Gregor whispered to Edgy, 'This is the top-flight wise woman you told me about?'

Edgy whispered to Gregor. 'She thinks with her teeth, that much is obvious.'

'What are you whispering about?' snapped Beryl.

'Quadraface harpies.'

'Glassers eh? Mythical as levy skeletons. They'll nip your head off with extraordinary ferocity.'

'My head? No . . .'

'Oh yes. Those bastards don't mess around.'

'Do you know how to survive them?

'I'm alive, aren't I?'

'I've no reason to suppose so.'

'Don't I bother you?'

'I see what you mean.' Edgy smiled. 'Well, you really are a font of wisdom.'

'Is that so, do I look like a font?'

Gregor pushed forward. 'Come on you old hag, you're wasting our time.'

'That has nothing to do with it. I'll break your legs! That's right, your legs!' And she began cackling and capering toward them in a scary way, all rags and elbows.

Gregor pulled at Edgy. 'Come on, we'll have to sort it on the fly.'

'Work out how to find and kill semi-transparent dragons on the fly?'

'I know – come on.'

Beryl kicked Edgy sharply in the balls and darted back up the slope, complaining at the assumption that she was wise. Seekers returning to civilisation would cover their embarrassment by inventing some arcane wisdom and attributing it to her. All she wanted was to be left alone.

'We'll tell one and all,' Edgy gasped, curled upon the ground, 'you have their best interests at heart. It'll be a blueprint for positive change.'

'Know what I think'd be a blueprint for positive change? You getting the hell away from me.' She snorted and gobbed a flob like an oyster.

'Just tell us where the harpies are,' Gregor stated, 'and we'll get out of your way.'

'You'll find them where you see the harpies which are called "quadraface".'

'Those are quadraface harpies,' Edgy wheezed.

'Oh yes, it'll work all right. I'm not even worried about that.'

Edgy staggered to his feet. 'You're . . . you're a moron.'

'So regret me.'

As they stumbled away, she called after them.

'Oh and mind how you go – some idiot released a 'gator out here.'

Haltingly chewing a sparrow behind locked doors and the hours of darkness, Max Gaffer sat in the Ultimatum Restaurant with only the head chef for company. 'I think I am correct in saying that a meal of this standard is a criminal offence. Saying thank you for it is like ceremonially forgiving the headsman before his work. I had no idea how much petrol you used here.'

Quandia Lucent stood over him. 'Condiments are necessary.'

Gaffer glanced at the menu again. 'Giblets parboiled for no reason, fluorite buns, armistice gutting, plasma earlobes, bladder walls tough as a belt, and on the back cover, a tamale erosion chart. This document is a disturbing reminder of mortality.'

'A formality,' the chef stated. 'It is not up to you.'

Gaffer dabbed his mouth with a rag, shaking his head in admiration. 'I'm reluctant to characterise it as a meal at all. You have quite an operation here, Mr Lucent. As Violaine said, "Cheese which, when sliced, can bend double without breaking, is likely not cheese." Let's go to chin level on this. You're hellbent for pasta saturation. I know you discourage other foodstuffs with a sneering expression and the propagation of this manner of incident.' He handed over a newspaper with the headline MINCE BINGE ENDS TRAGICALLY. 'In fact I like the way you think, so I'd like to help you. I happen to know that Barny Juno has been told everything there is to know about the edibility of oceanic fish and that he intends to pass on the knowledge.'

'Juno. He's the one who set free *una el crocodilia* in my restaurant, eh?'

'Yes, disgracefully, he probably did.'

The chef's expression became stormy. 'The fishes of the sea are a near-unending resource of non-pasta nutrition. Terrible, terrible.'

'I agree. Vertebrae like a zip fastener. Stay away.'

'Children know the purpose of food is decoration. That's why we discourage their attendance.'

'Look to Barny Juno, my friend. If you graft the pattern of change onto the pattern of fear, you'll find a match.'

A grim waiter stalked in with the next dish.

'Ah, doves,' said Gaffer, tucking in. 'Bounty of the sky.'

The first thing they captured was a vampire wearing some sort of apron – this they released in an embarrassment which kept them silent for half an hour.

Then they met the tiny Microlady, who lay in a palm bed and trilled of her peculiarities. 'I walk in shoes of eyelids,' she told them as they retreated through the contorted trees.

They even bumped into Fang, a zombie who worked with them in the sorting office and came out to the swamp to sleep in the damp earth. At their approach he arose yellow in rotted clothes, a corpse *par excellence*. 'Hey, Fang,' Edgy hailed him.

'What are you crazy guys doing this time?' Fang asked, his expression in trembling readiness for hilarity.

'Snaring glass harpies,' Edgy announced.

'Edgy's idea,' Gregor muttered.

The gristle man began baulking with laughter, his entire body jerking and folding. One strong convulsion threw his head from his shoulders and into the undergrowth – the cadaver sat back down as though stunned.

'I could use some coffee, and how,' said Edgy in a low, confidential tone as they moved on.

'The maples seem to have sprouted hind legs.'

'Shut up and help me with this,' said Edgy, unflapping a large map.

'You brought a Doggone Diagram here?'

'No, don't you recognise it? One of those old "Maps to the Morons" I used to sell. A guide to the homes of the biggest morons of our fair community. Doomed Eddie Gallo, GI Bill, Barny's house, your house, Prancer's room, Rudloe Manor, it's all here. Remember the time I told GI Bill he had something on his nose and he said it was just his head?' Edgy chuckled fondly.

'*My* house?'

'Anyway it's like I thought – the swamp's shown as just a random design at the map edge. No good for our purposes.'

'*My* house?'

Something knocked waves into the fog. Transparent channels were worming the atmosphere before Edgy's eyes. He halted Gregor and shrugged off his backpack. Casting an october switch before him, he watched it bounce in the air, spinning aside and landing in the brush. Then he unpacked a cornercage, placing it gently on the rumbling ground and unfolding a slip of paper. 'Listen, Round One,' he whispered. 'Cornercage Ltd instruction leaflet. "When someone must maintain a particular position, and that position cannot be maintained, the fixed need becomes a handle by which someone can be manipulated. Since the target entity must be invisible it will react to the knowledge of its visibility by hiding in our patented corner cage. Keep away from badgers."'

The switch deployed and two horse-sized dragons liquified a few feet in front of Edgy and Gregor.

'*My* house?'

'Focus, Round One. They're harpies, harpies. You knew that going in. Now don't make me come over there.'

Rills of shadow sawtoothed together and the earth was stamped to dust. Benthic light was flowing through the creatures' bodies and inside each ghosted the spirals of an abalone heart. These beauties had quadratic heads and flanks like shellac. 'Hello, harpies!' Edgy shouted at them, waving. 'I like what I see!'

One harpy bolted into the undergrowth, sprinting like a gazelle. The other panicked the other way, throwing itself at the cornercage. In a blaze of portable spinelight it was sucked into a space no bigger than a breadbin. 'Well,' chuffed Edgy, smiling stylish. '*Now* who's a danger to himself and others?'

7

A Change of Mind

Paranoia is an investment

Long reborn doom on the mat, first shadow of the day. The lips of the bed disengaging from sleepers over coffee. And as Gregor set up a video camera in his small bedroom in the hope of filming a few nap chickens, his friends gathered for wolf tart and tea in Snorters cafe. BB Henrietta frowned at the newspaper headline, GALLO SENSES FLOWER, above a picture of doomed Eddie Gallo looking at a flower. An embarrassed spokesman was claiming on Gallo's behalf that he was a veteran of nostril faith. 'That silence of white damnation, a handkerchief, will drown out his voice unless you vote, vote, vote for doomed Eddie Gallo!'

Edgy was displaying his novelty failings and the duelling scars of bad planning. 'I'm on to a king's ransom and a neglect to inform the relevant authorities.'

'Selling harpy meat?' BB scorned. 'It's a lame idea, alright? They'll hunt you down like a doll.'

'Is either of you eating this ultimate cracker?'

'So you think you're impressive now, brush head?'

'What's the point of hiding it? You know I reckon if the Steinway Spiders ever came back, I could tackle one.'

'Yeah, right,' BB snorted.

'Which gambit would you try?' Barny asked, with a marvelling stare.

'A running gambit,' Edgy declared.

'I favour a punching and screaming gambit for that kind of setup,' said BB Henrietta.

'With running at the end?'

'Optional.'

'Depending on the effectiveness of the punching and screaming.'

'Exactly.'

'Oh and we met Fang out there – that skinless wonder cracks me up very time.'

'You want some of this pasta salad, Edgy?'

'No thanks – I hate it.'

'Typical man – won't commit to a thing he doesn't want. What about you, Juno?'

'Maybe I should try eating a fish – EH Hunt keeps saying one of those things is the stuff of life. Gregor says he'll try it if I do first.'

'And acquaint yourselves with the toilet,' said BB.

'What Violaine said,' Barny stated, 'is that a toilet is like a fat ceramic swan in the bathroom. When did it arrive and why is it there? Answers on a postcard.'

'On a what?' Edgy asked.

'It's just an expression, I think.'

'Other than you poisoning yourself, Bubba,' BB said, 'what have you been up to?'

'The shaman says I should defeat the monster in my dreams and everything'll be alright,' said Barny without enthusiasm.

'Hmm. That'd work well in my Miasma play. Framed narrative.'

'Well, listen, Beltane is good,' Edgy agreed, 'but he can't hold a candle to Feral Beryl.'

'Alright, harpy whisperer,' BB asked, dripping with sarcasm, 'what did she say?'

'Eh?' Edgy jittered, taken by surprise. 'Well, she said some very important advice actually. Er, for us all. Yes, she said, these pearly words here: "Problems are like dogs – they stare, they demand to be fed, they spin in place".'

'I think I see that bullshit borealis Gregor's always talking about.'

'You dare? Can you perceive what I've done? Can, can, do you know how I fought that quadraface fiend to the floor? You're looking at a man reared on the following: stares, palping, a tawny scab, metallic mouths in a bottomless lake, collars, parlour tricks gone awry, and crazy talk.'

His claim was met with a revolted silence.

Edgy continued, equable in his joy. 'I'm thinking of changing my name to Bollard Salvo, what do you reckon? And wearing antlers like candlestick holders.'

'I think you're getting a little carried away.'

'Imagine being announced and making an entrance!'

Edgy pulled a face which was, regrettably, attached to a passer-by. 'Reality can polish my arse!' And he began shuddering in his seat, foam flying from his mouth.

BB turned to Barny. 'You know, Juno, you're a gormless idiot but at least you never go into violent convulsions. And that's cool in its way.'

'I don't know what you mean.'

'Right.'

The Mayor was again posing on a high horse. He exhibited his chins like a flow chart. The painter looked upon the image which had filled his canvas – that of a sleepy gibbon in a shredded undershirt.

The door flashed open and Gaffer burst into the office already laughing. 'A reply from the circus. Delivered by some sort of winged midget.'

'What now,' sighed the Mayor, bored.

'It says "I would rather burst my own nose than enter Accomplice in time for your jaundice exhibition. Arriving too late to be of any use, we will expose you to the greatest spectacle ever seen. And be assured, Mayor, I will bare my wonderful arse also to the town. Signed, Karloff Velocet, Fall Marshall, Circus of the Heart's Shell."'

'Is that all? Where have you been?'

'You've no right to time my entertainment.'

'You look rejuvenated.'

'An abstract term for saying you hate my jacket.'

'Why does everything have to be about your underwear?'

'I never mentioned it.'

'No you didn't.' Mayor Rudloe looked suspicious. He gestured at the painter. 'You can bring your waves of desperation back with you tomorrow.' When the painter had left with his equipment, Rudloe dismounted and approached Max Gaffer. 'This sudden-death integrity of yours, what's it all about?'

'I considered mercy. I stopped trying with the realisation that even the greatest show of it isn't fun. Confusion sometimes contracts rewards. You gave me the treat too soon.'

'What the hell's going on around here?' Rudloe demanded, his face congested with anger. 'Just do your job and enumerate the fancy misgivings you're famous for.'

'Very well – Barny Juno.'

'Juno? Rode in here on a swan, that's the trouble.'

'Indeed. I've corralled the great and the good against him. They'll use his blank face as a broom for the township.'

'Without consulting me? *My* arse is the engine room of this community. Mine. What if he was denounced by a pig made of straw, with a tape recorder hidden inside?'

'It would give the term "false conspirator" new meaning, plus amusement to all. No need to disturb the natural order.'

'If they need order, show them the door. A large rectangle is guaranteed to give a good example. Then keep 'em busy about the Miasma. It's their perfect opportunity to avoid acknowledging they don't really care much anyway.' Rudloe sparked his cigar with a lighter the size of a car battery.

'Your lungs must be black as a wallet.'

'And your heart must be large as a grape, lawyer. What other business?'

'The fugitive doll. Sanctuaries seem to bang open like greyhound traps for that one. I recommend that it's dispatched before the Miasma.'

'Agreed. Can't have a jangly marionette twitching against the revellers can we. Order the Brigade be released. Anything else?'

'Can I speak freely sir? You know there's folk running blood stills out in the swamp to make account for the levy.'

'I've been carefully ignoring the fact for years, why bring it up now?'

'Because if that slubby cabal the Conglomerate were to learn that they were often feeding on cloned blood, that you were laughing at them behind their collective back . . .'

'Who'd tell them?'

'Let's just say that if you want to spring from this window here onto the jagged face of an onlooker, I won't stand in your way.'

'It's a high window, and not a round one.'

'All true. Is this your only comment?'

Rudloe's face sort of grimaced with affront, his nose and gob jockeying for position. 'Have a care, Gaffer. These damn fool comments could bring your gummy ballet of a career to an end. I think I'm numbered among the Conglomerate's closest confidants.'

'Your days, if not yourself.'

'What's that?'

'Nothing – I have a case to prepare. I'll dispose of Barny Juno if you can't. Good day.'

'Oh good day. And don't let the door flume into infernal meat and flip you screaming to hell on the way out.'

Not noticing a floor lobster on the desk, Rudloe snatched it up when the phone rang. He barked hello and the creature scuttled against his face. 'Bloody hell!' he screamed, and hurled the clattery vermin through the balcony window.

'Where this arrow lands,' proclaimed the trickster Prancer Diego to some children in the Square. 'I shall learn braille.'

And he fired the arrow in the air, watching it hit a flying floor lobster in a small explosion of meat.

The Brigade approached Kenny Reactor's farm armed to the teeth with knives, spiked maces and an october switch. The sarge halted them at the gate, primed the switch, and looked across the head field, fondling a thin badge made of a dog's nose-leather. Finished, he turned to his deputy, who brandished a dish.

'Snail, sarge?'

'Don't mind if I do. What are they?'

'Snails, sarge.'

'Snails. Don't mind if I do.'

'Get your face round that then.'

'What is it.'

'A snail, sarge.'

'Snail. Alright then. Eat it do I?'

'Eat it sarge, that's right.'

'What is it?'

'Snail – a snail, sarge.'

'Snail.'

'A snail, sarge. See? It's a snail.'

'Snail is it. Well now.'

'Snail.'

'Snail, eh. Well, don't mind if I do.'

'Good on yuh.'

'Right.'

'You eatin' it then?'

'Eh?'

'You eatin' that?'

'What is it?'

Before the deputy could reply, a peal of firecrackers announced the approach of a group of Fuseheads. 'Are you the Belly Honour Guard?' sneered the front man, and the others cackled like tarts.

'And who might you be?'

'We seek the Church of Automata's escaped abomination, you bastard,' announced the front man.

The sarge smirked aside to his deputy. 'Notice how he called me a bastard? Everyone calls me that round here.'

'Remember the hedgehogs we saw here last time, sarge?' said Gibbs, looking into a hedgerow. 'They've given birth to hoglets.'

'What's the matter with you people?' asked a cannon worshipper, indignant. He addressed a colleague. 'Bring the switch – we'll root out the walking blasphemy without help from these.'

'Look sarge, somebody gave me, ah, a drawing of a hoglet.'

'Nobody gave you a drawing of a hoglet, Perkins,' said the sarge, smirking. 'You drew a hoglet, didn't you?'

'Okay, sarge, I did.'

'It's good.'

'Forget these jokers – the sooner we catch the doll, the sooner we celebrate. Onward!'

'Another hoglet appeared in the picture, sarge,' said Perkins, his face smudged with ink. 'It's incredible.'

The Cannonites pushed past the Brigade into the head field, knocking the october switch from the sarge's hands. Activating, it threw the field into acidic negative. The doll Maquette was buried to the neck among the heads, topped with a grubby fright wig – she was noticeable for a split second before the fuseheads dropped their own switch and neutralised the first.

But neither group had noticed the doll, and when the sarge ordered Ripper to unpack the picnic gear, no one could really be bothered to carry on the search. The sarge showed everyone how to draw hedgehogs starting from the stubby nose. One of the Fuseheads explained how he had simultaneously grown two overlapping beards, quite distinct from each other. Someone played a flute.

Shadowed by a nearby tree, Distaff Plastique was stood waxenly, like a totem, its skin earth red. It was mid-afternoon before the happy group dispersed, heading for the beach. Distaff stepped onto the field, kicking mechanically through vegetable heads.

A thing of fright paint and disordered hair, Maquette was struggling out of the ground like a newborn, blankly frantic as the automatic man approached. As she freed herself and began tick-tocking toward the gate, she looked backward to see Distaff halt abruptly. After a minute this strange, cored servant turned around, an earth fork hanging from its back like a tow pike. Kenny Reactor stood beyond it, startled by his own act.

Kenny bolted in one direction, Maquette in another. Distaff Plastique followed the doll north.

Something woke Gregor – he had to go see the lawyer, he remembered. He felt terrible, like someone had worn him for a hat. He reached the offices of De'ath and Destruction to regard his counsel raggedly through bloodshot eyes. A dark suit full of dead nerves, De'ath was immaculately unimaginative. No air had ever gotten in or out. 'Ah, the hardy loser,' he greeted Gregor.

'Is something wrong?'

'That will do. The appearance is many months away. We merely need to play out the grim scenario ahead of time. Remember, the question is not whether a thing is true – the question is what number of human beings are prepared to accept it as a possibility. Regrettably, the burden of proof that you're a normal fella rests entirely with you and your reactions in court. It is impossible to imagine how they could come to view you with any favour. This flimsy vapour you call an alibi – what was it again?'

'I was at the slaughterhouse.'

'Oh, that's just dandy. Your honour, my client couldn't have done the murder because he was at the slaughterhouse. My god.'

'What do you want me to say to you.'

'What you say to me sonny jim is neither here nor there – you can tell me you were kissing a badger and loving every minute of it. But in court laddie, in court you're obliged to at least try.'

'I don't know the form. Do I wear trousers there.'

'Christ, yes.'

'And a tie?'

'Yes, yes. And you tell them you were in a bar with eighty other people, all of them as pure as yourself. That's the way.'

'So you want me to charm the pants off them?'

'If you can. Though quite frankly, my boy, I doubt you could charm a dead wren off a hedge.'

'Did you say murder? I never murdered anyone.'

'Ah yes, some sort of public abomination wasn't it? Either way you're headed for a room with a drain in the middle, if you get my drift.'

'So it's all decided.'

'Nonsense, we are free to be laden with proof on the matter.'

'Isn't there any way out?'

'Let's see. Teeth clamped hard to the judge may cause an adjournment I suppose. He's quite brittle.' And De'ath opened the large cabinet to view the pupating judge. A seed once the size and weight of an owl had already developed into the full-sized drylord which would, when its eyes were slit awake, sit in judgement upon Gregor. 'And this message Max Gaffer brought me earlier might have something useful to say.' He unwrapped the missive and read it silently, then looked up at Gregor. 'My prayers are with you and your monstrous friends.'

'What? Why?'

'No sentiment or waste will force its way into my account. The trial is on for tomorrow. Apparently the courthouse has grown at unprecedented speed.'

'What? Death! What are we gonna do?'

'Listen carefully, Gregor. One of the big guns in the court's armoury is its sedative effect. Bigger is its dismissal of objective reality and biggest, its ability to abduct people without moving a muscle – the abductees do all the work, tranced by assumed authority. I love it.' And ropes of drool began lengthening from the lawyer's gob.

'What's the best I can get away with?'

'The best? It'll be on your permanent record.'

'Permanent?'

In Snorters cafe later that day Gregor raved at Edgy about the concept. 'I never thought I'd make a mark – everything is transitory, I thought. I'd die, be forgotten.'

'Right.'

'But this thing – my "permanent record", Edge. Permanent. He insists that people'll know about me forever.'

'Know that you had sex with a mechanical statue.'

'What's the difference? He said forever, he insisted on it. Apparently this is the one thing that survives beyond the end of everything – you gotta give it a go, right?'

'I think it's an exaggeration, Round One. The record doesn't last forever.'

'Then why would I give a damn about it? This guy stood there being very precise about the whole procedure. I've created something permanent!'

And Gregor went home swinging each leg forward lustily, down into his little room where he slapped the nap chickens video into the machine and popped a beer.

The edit swarm coalesced into the image of the Round One bent in bed, his face slack. Presently, the ventilation grille on the wall swung open and a stubby leg reached through, and another. A mechanical doll, its face painted up like a clown, stood into the room and looked at the sleeping Gregor. Then it dashed silently off-screen. A dark arm angled out of the vent and pulled after it a large moulded plastic man, which straightened up and marched immediately out of view.

Max Gaffer decended into the gutty dungeon concealed beneath the Blood Shed. The clammy air and lambent red atmosphere hit him – wet fungal walls pulsed with fanned capillaries, a tongue swung in the clock and the chamber was filled with a wall-to-wall meat morass, multi-mouthed and occupied. 'The only thing on this list I recognise is the Wesley Kern gun.'

'But where did Turbot get it?' a larger mouth croaked. 'It's not his handwriting.'

'It's signed "Low".'

'There's no Low on the mug levy register. This is a waste of our sweet, sweet time. Now concerning unproven heifers . . .'

Another mouth interrupted. 'We have a visitor.' Lime eyes opened in the dark. 'Look at him, pretending he feels no disgust.'

A flesh turret of sneers projected from the upper surface of the Conglomerate. 'What makes the Mayor's errand boy so forward of a sudden?'

'I have a strange live medallion in my chest which directs my actions.'

'If you weren't a lawyer you'd know that was your heart.'

Gaffer opened his shirt to display the toroidal fitting from which the infernal drillbit emerged.

'You could hang furry dice on that, as on your career to date. You wish to advance? Is this your bid to avoid an eiderdown death away from the cameras? Armageddon goodies your prize? A real polecat rush for the glory. We understand. Benevolence is the first chapter in a boring book.'

'Mayor Rudloe is wealthy and slow,' said Gaffer, 'dull but loyal. I expect he's back at the office now, frantically throwing phones on the fire. But you could do better.'

'You've done well yourself, amid a form of politics advertised on pencils. In a very real way, it does you credit.'

'I'll take that remark to the bank and see what transpires.'

'You will apologise first.'

The stern resolve drained from Gaffer's slackening face. 'I . . . draw a line under what I said.'

'Funny.'

'I never laugh so hard that I can't talk money.'

'You know the difference between a primitive woodsman and a politician, Gaffer?'

'One chops his quivers, and the other—'

'The difference,' the Conglomerate interrupted, 'is that one will hesitate before touting any given concern in return for pay.'

'Why have the people ever believed that all the blood they give goes to work the town clock?'

'People will do almost anything to avoid acknowledging that they're powerless. That's a sturdy handle.' A loose arm tapped one of the gore-gummed sump valves in the wall. 'There's another exaction coming up, you'll see even the oldsters struggling out of the swamps to get bled. The agitator Wesley Kern's been silky dust these many years. I believe an excavation was completed recently in the walls of the skeleton coast. Seventeen tons of pocket fluff was found in the cave. It seems your ancestors were as boring as you are.'

'Have you heard of a Varney bug, Mr Gaffer?'

This mouth was no more than a palping spout which Gaffer doubted he could ever get used to.

'No sir, I haven't.'

'It's like a floor lobster, but it births directly and physically from the originator's head. If the corrupt fellow survives, he's much the worse for wear. Be careful your plan doesn't kill you birthing, Gaffer.'

Gaffer looked at the lung-hung ceiling and skids of red tar, the moving meat amid vapour. 'The enemy of uncertainty might think the answer lies in grammar,' he observed. Varicose alarm wires bloated the walls, going to his head. 'Progress is formidable on short acquaintance – after a time its existence can't even be proven.'

For years Mike Abblatia had been living an extra day between Thursday and Friday, growing a little older than his years. Though supposedly a young man, his back ached and seemed to swell more with every vehicle that was stolen during his watch.

Abblatia worked at Spacey's gas station. He sat on the forecourt next to a tank marked Zapata Oil, eating a sandwich and contemplating the horizon. He had the notion that people lived in a sandwich, moving always between the earth and sky. Rooms, roads, buildings, all were horizontal strips. Death was when a person fell out of the sandwich.

A false child, fresh out of some specialist foundry, wandered across the forecourt toward him. Its head was like a dirty kettle and its gob was like a pedal-bin. She waddled over, looked at him awhile and then sat down on some mixed ash-and-bone blocks. They looked across the scorched tarmac in the quiet of the afternoon. The forecourt was edged with a few wooden posts and loopy elaborate flowers, some like hang-peeled bananas. The gas stands were rusted and reversed into complicated colours.

Abblatia was so attuned to mechanisms he could hear a watch ticking in the stomach of a dog. The mannequin had solid glass eyes and a heart like a pascaline. She was lonely. Surely somewhere there was a blued steel boy for her to click around with.

Abblatia took up a boxy bottle of water and drank, then offered it to the imp. She was gone. A minute later he heard tyres sizzling over gravel – a truck drove around the station and swerved into the lane, the doll at the wheel.

8

Let us Lurk

A man who cannot be changed has no need to fight

After creating several vats of glue, Verbal had consulted the chef Quandia Lucent on the constituents for pasta. The chef informed him he had been mixing the quantities correctly – the difference was only one of definition.

And so, as everyone entered the courtroom, they found it a brittle venue indeed. In place of the crossbone masonry usually deployed for perjury reverberation there were bland starch walls wormed with spaghetti filigree. Instead of torsons and flexions of bone there were volutes of pasta and exquisitely turned fusilli banisters. Lanceolate pinnacles of macaroni jutted dryly at the sky. There were some token pillars of poured bone which didn't reach the ceiling, and what appeared to be hairline cracks in the walls were actually fine print.

Meanwhile the drylord was as complete as it would ever be. Uncertain as to how many nostrils it would require to convey a bearing of authority, it had overcompensated, vacillated and finally abandoned the matter as it now stood. It had a hundred and twenty, so its nose resembled a piece of sponge. Yet, despite all this, it didn't seem to be alive, propped at the courtroom's head like a Guy Fawkes.

'That frail catnip judge over there,' whispered De'ath as he and Gregor entered the courtroom, 'is the ramp to respectability.'

In discussing strategy with De'ath, Gregor had remarked that it wouldn't hurt to give the judge the cake they had stowed in the cupboard a few days before. But De'ath had wavered, stating that it would be too obvious an attempt to curry favour with the court. Gregor had suggested that openly poisoning the cake would neutralise this impression and the lawyer had agreed to the remedy.

De'ath handed it over. 'A gift, your honour, as befits a man in your ridiculous situation.'

'You think you can curry favour with this sugary fondant creation?'

Gregor laughed lightly. 'No, your honour – in fact the cake is poisoned with a variety of household detergents. Testament to my indifference to your opinion.'

'What?'

'What my client meant to say,' stammered De'ath, 'is that he has no desire to influence you favourably.'

'Having offered me poison cake in the courtroom, I think he can rest assured on that score.'

'Trying to sway the dry reed of the judge?' announced Max Gaffer, beaming as he entered. 'Send a message, judge, if you can.'

'You put this on the fast track,' De'ath declared to Gaffer.

'Still feels deadly slow though, doesn't it?'

'He's right,' said Gregor, surprised at the realisation. 'How do they do that?'

'I've explained before,' hissed De'ath, pushing Gregor away from the laughing Gaffer and on to the bench. 'Now sit there, stay silent and for god's sake remember how daft you are.'

De'ath reached into the black petals of an open bag, retrieving dozens of prematurely aged files as spectators filed into the gallery. Half of Accomplice was here, including Barny and the gang. The jury meanwhile consisted of twelve heads on a trolley. A distorted outcome was ensured by the fact that this was the only time their opinions would be allowed to affect anything.

Gaffer was wearing his eyes swept back these days and compared to De'ath he was slick as a wolf, all blade suit and cufflinks of pink flesh. He called Gregor to the stand. 'Let us dispense first with those events which are a matter of record. Did you not, during the course of the Mayor's "You Want a Piece of Me?" speech, crouch out upon the ornate ledge and dispense sexual favours galore upon a paint-flaking statue which formed a part of the town clock mechanism.'

Gregor looked over at De'ath.

'Don't expect any help from this conjuror's stooge you call a lawyer,' said Gaffer, 'who for years has been throwing good alibis after bad. Confess with grace, at least.'

Gregor tried to appear unconcerned, his head repeatedly lolling forward as though he were nodding off. He had asked Barny how to manage it, and Barny had advised him to 'look to the giraffe', showing Gregor a picture of a giraffe and explaining the animal's beautiful neck motion. Gregor knew that to convey the action as a visual soundbite he had to speed it up, so now his head was shooting back and forth in a shocking manner. Some of the spectators screamed with a kind of primal terror but Gaffer seemed to understand. 'Let the record show that the defendant has given a greatly accelerated impersonation of a giraffe.' He retrieved an exhibit. 'I have here a photograph of a tumescent tearaway assaulting our communal timepiece.' Gaffer glanced at it negligently, then brandished it at Gregor. 'Do you recognise the spud-like figure in this picture?' There was a pause. 'May the record reflect that the defendant has indicated his own face. And attempted a questioning, bland expression.' Gaffer replaced the exhibit. 'In fact you're not particular what you do, are you? The sort of fella who doesn't really need a reason, eh? So you decided to whip it out and see how much trouble it could handle? I wonder, how do people get this way? A single wrong turn in life and – bang – it's ledge-climbing and statue assault. This urge – let's call it "Hell Frenzy" – it was perhaps also the cause of that little case of Stegosaurus Interruptus in the bone museum a few months ago.'

'It was a Triceratops,' Gregor muttered feebly.

'A Tops eh? And you . . .' – Gaffer consulted a file – ' "erupted from its skull and scared the children".'

'They were there to learn,' Gregor protested.

'I wish I could believe that,' said Gaffer sadly. 'Were you not in fact on a burgling spree when you went into Hell Frenzy? Do you claim never to have stuffed yourself through a stranger's window and collected certain of their belongings according to a dog-eared list given you by the devil himself?

It was the rule that during the first cross the performing lawyer should slow his breath to imperceptibility in emulation of the living dead, and the lawyer seated should hold his breath entirely, so that the more continent a lawyer was about his objections the more comical he seemed. De'ath had been sitting for several minutes, cheeks full, face turning crimson, and when he finally bolted to his feet to yell 'Objection' it was a garbled explosion from a gasping figure who smashed through the fragile panelling and staggered to his knees with a wretching sob.

Gaffer eyed De'ath disdainfully. 'Nothing further.'

De'ath stood slowly and straightened his tie. He seemed subdued as he approached the witness stand. 'You've been a moron how long?'

'Twenty-eight years.'

'Okay, alright . . . And for that period you have suffered from trovander, a statue-related illness.'

Gaffer stood, breathing heavily. 'Your honour, m'colleague's an unprecedented idiot and I never tire of his failings – guard your faces when this one's learning to use a fork. But the illness gambit he just exposed us to leads us all astray, leaving us finally exhausted, dehydrated and terrified.'

'It goes to the question of insanity, your honour.'

'Whose, you bastard? Don't touch that!' The drylord yanked his gavel from De'ath's convulsive grasp. 'What's the matter with you?'

De'ath returned to the witness. 'So, a sickness. Then your expression of these lusts was . . . curative?'

'I have no idea,' stated Gregor simply.

'You're giving me every reason to believe that it was a medical compulsion. So that occasion on the belfry was a real red letter day for you.'

'Red what?'

'Finally – I now find I can no longer refute the fact that you were a sick man when you molested the inanimate figurine on the ledge. I see undeniably now that you made yourself a hostage to fortune by displaying your wares to the town – yet your generosity is today so shabbily abused. Let us not assassinate this lad further, your honour. We have done enough. Have we no sense of decency, sir, at long last? Have we left no sense of decency?'

The first of a series of noxious gasses was pumped into the courtroom, causing nausea and heavy delirium. When the air had cleared a little, Max Gaffer was cross-examining his second witness. 'Your name is Plantin Edge.'

'No sir.'

'No?'

'No, well, my name is Bollard Salvo.'

'Bollard Salvo, is that right.'

'Bollard Salvo yes sir, born and raised, more every day.'

'Where did I get,' Gaffer scrutinised a file, 'Plantin Edge?'

'Well, that's my name.' Edgy instantly regretted his words. 'Damn I was so close! Bubba, you see that? Maybe the antlers . . .'

Edgy produced a double candlestick holder and put it carefully on his head. De'ath groaned, whispering aside to Gregor. 'Your friend's delicate balancing act has had the effect of giving his face a look of wariness and worry. Nobody will trust him now.'

'What's that yellow slime all over you?' Gaffer demanded.

'Well it's actually blood. When I was called on so unexpectedly, I was in the middle of cutting up a body.'

'What kind of body?'

'A quadraface harpy. The meat's semi-transparent like pearl.'

'Isn't that illegal?'

'It . . . would be if I weren't joking. I was actually baking a lemon meringue, as I always do on a Tuesday.'

'This is Wednesday.'

'Then the meringue is burning. Excuse me.'

'Wait a minute, you're not going anywhere. Did you witness the defendant assaulting a public marionette?'

'If I did, this is hardly the time or place to discuss it.'

'Brilliant denying, Mr Edge. Don't smile. What is your relationship to this flabby envoy from hell?'

Edgy attempted a suave demeanour. 'Well he's a friend, a work colleague, and latterly a student in the art of lurking. I can see your surprise – perhaps even shock? You see, after Gregor was accused of waving his trouble monkey at the Mayor during another speech – I think it was the "I Need More of Your Sweet Blood" monologue – he was fired from the sorting office where he also lived and, for a while, had to stay with me in the Bata Motel where I evade the rent by pretending to be a ghost.'

'You witnessed this previous outrage during another speech?'

'Yes, I was wearing only a sheet, I recall, which was torn away leaving me to slap home naked except for the context I kept explaining.'

Gaffer fixed the jury with a glare. 'Naked, ladies and gentlemen.' He turned back to Edgy. 'Have there been other such incidents involving the defendant?'

'Well, it's funny you should mention that,' Edgy chuckled. 'We were in the Dummy Garden the other day, and Round One here, he starts in on his own statue.'

There were gasps of shock and efforting imagination from the audience.

'It must have been an interesting sensation,' Edgy laughed. 'Like being covered in glitter glue.'

Gaffer, smiling ruefully amid the disturbance, ended his questioning and De'ath stood. 'Mr Edge,' De'ath shouted a little for silence. 'You claim to work at the sorting office. What do you do there?'

'Well,' Edgy swallowed, 'like it says, we sort things. Some goes in the trash, some is, er . . . burnt.'

'In which case, why must you evade rent? You are paid, yes?'

'Well, I think I speak for us all when I say I've better things to spend my wages on than mere rent. In any case, I don't always go in. I have a hammock which I enjoy. I'm a beautiful man, as you can see. I believe it was Violaine who said, "Since my very being is involuntary, isn't also everything it contains?".'

'The human stage is not suitable for hammocks. Idleness is an insurmountable barrier.'

'What of it, if it keeps out whatever beast it was built for.'

'Your honour, I move to strike this witness—'

'Hold him back!' shouted the judge as De'ath sprang toward the flinching Edgy. Three ushers grabbed the lawyer and pulled him to the floor.

'And here we have the unlikely kingpin of the operation,' Gaffer stated when Barny was called to the stand. 'Yes, looks like a living child doesn't he? Yet the fact that he knows and is known to every principal player in this deadly game is far from coincidental. If history teaches us nothing, it is that Barny Juno is a demon from screaming hell. Mr Juno, sinister alias "Juniper", is it not the case that you are acquainted with the defendant, *and* with Plantin Edge?'

'Yes, ma'am.'

'You entered a soup kitchen with Plantin Edge and committed . . . assault with a deadly leopard wasn't it?'

'Edgy rode the leopard – I was upon my fine lion, Mister Braintree.'

'The same lion which ate a tailor and attacked a dactylian fiend bent on mayhem. Indeed your home is packed to the twisted rafters with winged and stepping animals, isn't it?'

'They're my friends. I rescued Mister Braintree from the circus. A healthy predator is a happy predator.'

'Happy predator,' Gaffer repeated with heavy inflection. 'You have eight hundred eels in your garden – does that sound like the behaviour of a responsible man?'

'No, I suppose it doesn't, does it? Eels, are they? Are there really eight hundred?'

'Eight hundred eels.'

'Eight hundred.'

'Does that surprise you?'

'It interests me. I didn't know there were any. That's fantastic. Is there any water back there?'

'I don't know.'

'But you've seen the eels?'

De'ath bolted to his feet. 'He's got you on the run, Gaffer!'

'Everyone's seen the eels,' Gaffer declared with lofty patience, rolling his eyes to the ceiling.

'Who's seen these supposed eels?' shouted De'ath. 'Who, in this courtroom?'

'The eels have never been in this courtroom and thus have never been seen here,' Gaffer stated as though explaining all to a child.

'Is that so?' yelled De'ath, pulling eel after eel from his jacket and flinging them at Gaffer and the startled jury. 'An eel, an eel, an eel!'

'And so,' stated Gaffer, flicking an eel from his shoulder, 'you have conveniently proven that everyone in this courtroom has seen the eels.'

De'ath sank slowly into his seat again.

Gaffer swiped up a document with a flourish. 'And I have here a list of Juno's trespasses which I will shovel into everyone's ears now. He set a lion upon a tailor; released a swarm of bees in a laundry; drew a massive picture of an exploding arse on the landscape; pretended he could fly but chose not to; built and released a mechanical child upon the town; interrupted a cat in mid-yawn, particularly despicable; wore a blanket round his face and peered out of it all cute like a baby; held a funeral for a lizard and dropped his pants during the eulogy; passed a scribbled note to a duck on a pond, after which the duck swam away and was never seen again; claimed he was too exhausted to flirt; backed over an old wooden radio with a tractor. As we can see, his face is flawed and simplistic. He cannot speak of the sun or sky without making it transparently clear that he resents their achievements and abilities. And apparently he blames it all on some massive demonic insect with a brain the size of an engine block.'

Woozy with indifference, Barny began to nod.

'Let's get to the heart of the wash, shall we? Our community is in crisis, its particular chaos threatened by an organising force which seeks to guide it like a lamb to armageddon. Do we really believe the logistical smarts originate with this champion idiot?' He pointed at Gregor.

And then to the stand came a rogue's gallery of friends and acquaintances. BB Henrietta described Barny as 'failure bait' and started laughing so hard her hair caught fire.

Official records were silent on the question of Sags Dumbar's plasmate head, which lolled sideways like a bag of water. 'I believe you work with this walking lens fault?' Gaffer asked of Barny.

'I'll have the roast beef platter,' said Sags, and nothing more.

Fang took the stand wearing a strange wicker jacket designed to retain his tripes. His face hung away in three ragged strips. De'ath hissed aside to Gregor. 'Is there any hope, indeed life, in this walking autopsy?'

Gregor leaned to whisper. 'No.'

'Mr Fang,' Gaffer began.

'Just . . . Fang,' gurgled the cadaver.

'Fang then. Can you explain how it is that Barny Juno knows so many of the slovenly, the criminal, the sick and the insane?'

'He lucked out,' came the response from a mouth which had seen better days. 'Chum.'

'Don't call me "chum".' Gaffer turned toward Barny. 'Not what you'd call a good account from this royally rotten friend of yours.'

'What do you expect?' said Barny. 'He hides in the mud.'

Completely phased by the reply, Gaffer camouflaged his frown by repeatedly muttering 'Such a macabre retinue', but everyone thought he was saying 'Suck my carburettor nude' and it was a while before procedure was re-established.

Barny's boss, the Captain, was grilled to within an inch of his life as to the purpose of the sorting office, until his panicked dissembling fragmented into wracking, hysterical sobs and he was led gently from the courtroom.

Mr Peterson merely claimed that Barny had a 'cock the size of a draft log' which had to be 'kept under a tarp'.

De'ath finally found his voice, and stood proud. 'Your honour, this witness is rubbish.'

'I'll need a technical objection, Mr De'ath.'

'Very well, I suppose, it's just occurred to me that since Mr Peterson owns the hydroponics plant, he effectively owns this jury of vegetable heads.'

'That's actually rather good,' frowned the drylord.

'I must admit I sounded more confident than I felt,' chuckled De'ath.

The final witness was Mayor Rudloe, who was still trying to pull on his containment suit as he was marched into the courtroom. 'Exposure!' he gasped, seeing the assembled masses, and attempted to zip his hood as he was forced to the stand. 'Adopt explanation demeanour, Gaffer,' he demanded.

'After all,' the lawyer stated smoothly, 'there can be no doubt about your part in this. You were on the balcony above the town clock when the molestation occurred.'

'I well remember the incident, so what? I was informing the town I'd rule dead-eyed and bloated from atop a hill of human skulls and then all hell broke loose in the bell chamber.'

'Oh, now – even to an unattentive listening your account is an obvious lie.'

'Eh?'

'The evil genius Barny Juno – he's known to you?'

'Yes, he's the fellow who entered my office dressed as a grizzly, flew past the window on a swan, whipped me with a python and asked for a job.'

'And what purpose is served by the blood tax? Where does it all go?'

'What? The levy? Well, it drives the blood clock, as you well know.'

'So much? Many suspect that the bulk goes elsewhere.'

'You work in my office, Gaffer – if it did, you'd know it.'

'Indeed,' said Gaffer.

'And be implicated,' added Rudloe in a hurry. 'In any case the evidence for that is entirely anecdotal.'

'So's your own account of yourself, the world and anything you've ever experienced.'

'Blackmail and insurrection,' stated the Mayor, thought-fully. 'Here, among the dead.'

'Perhaps I should leave you here.'

The Mayor stared at him levelly. 'You assume too much.'

'I'm finished with this one, your honour,' said Gaffer dismissively, and turned away.

'Your honour,' De'ath announced as the Mayor stood down, 'I'd like to introduce a surprise witness, but since I don't have one, I'm placing a set of false gums on the front of the witness stand.'

'So I see. Does this mean anything?'

'I'm thinking about that.' De'ath frowned down at his shoes for a while.

'Anything yet?' asked the judge.

'No.'

'I'm going to have to hurry you.'

'Well, since you pressure me, let's just say it means . . . nothing unusual.'

'You can take the gums away now, counsellor.'

'Well alright, but I'm not happy.'

Kenny Reactor spritzed water over the jury heads during a short recess, the ash of innocents was spread on the floor and Dumbar's gelid head was the talk of the time lounge. The court resumed for closing statements.

De'ath strode slowly about the court, his words a steady drip. 'You have seen a series of witnesses, real and imagined, go on at length about my client's depravities, as well as sundry unrelated matters designed to stun us with boredom, dulling the senses and stripping the myelin from our finer nerves. But I'm not so sure. Look at the accused now, for perhaps the last time. He has a face that sets back the cause of civilisation a hundred years. His ears can open and close like a valve and he makes a virtue of admitting it. The days of the week are his personal disaster in serial form. Yet Gregor here, a pioneer of sorts, explores for us the byways of sensuality and should be applauded. His blink-and-you'll miss-it sanity, meanwhile, should provoke our tears, not our scorn. This offence, witnessed by so many people and from such a variety of angles that a 360 degree hologram of the incident has already been mass-produced and is on sale on the very steps of this court, is not beyond pardon. I myself once rogered a standing cow and the pleasure it afforded me is beyond the scope of this closing argument to describe, even in outline. No, ladies and gentlemen of the jury, I cannot do it justice – but your duty today is to do justice to the twenty-four-hour erotic holocaust who sits before us. He refused to be furtive, and that's how matters stand.'

Max Gaffer's statement was more folksy, appealing to common sense and a desire for slowly revolving gore.

'That one over there,' he began, pointing to Gregor, 'that's what we're dealing with – pear shaped and he doesn't care. Every time he opens his distorted mouth, we are witness to a turmoil of crinkle-cut alibis and mind-boggling profanity. Nothing pleases him more than to disgrace himself in the public square. If he does not ride upon dogs it is only because he has no wish to do so. And since I was exposed to his excuses my forehead has taken on the consistency of tough leather. Yes, ladies and gentlemen, we have all had to suffer the poorest of explanations from defence counsel as to why this little universe of darkness forced his attentions upon a defenceless effigy. You have seen Mr De'ath attempt to discredit the witness Plantin Edge by smacking him in the mouth. Another witness, the one wearing Jonathan glasses, has been ejected on a clever technicality. All designed to deflect attention away from the ringleader. Because such events don't occur by chance, my friends. In a random world, the organising hand stands out like a snorting pig in a smashed wedding cake. As Violaine said, "Some wait to be discovered – others, to be found out." Barny Juno, that featherheaded wonder-child in the gallery, purporting to be a simple man, committed clear-cut lurking during the assault, looking on, knowing, seeing, breathing. He was a confidant of all the key agents, and a sworn enemy of the Mayor. With so much evidence, condemning this man has never been easier. And I have here a sworn affidavit, signed by one hundred people, stating that they saw Juno ordering Gregor to disrupt the Mayor's speech and subsequently shouting "Hooray, I am a sinister presence".'

'I wish Chloe was here,' said Barny in the spectators' gallery. 'I love her so much, Edgy.'

'Bubba,' Edgy hushed urgently. 'They've got it in for you.'

A couple of chefs in the row in front turned back with glares of approbation.

'Pass that up,' the judge ordered, and Gaffer gave him the document. 'How can we know these forged signatures are real?'

Max Gaffer pushed forward a barrow of stacked papers. He took a sheet from the top. 'This is a sworn affidavit attesting to the authenticity of the signatures on the first document. This is signed by a different bunch of people.'

'How do we know those signatures are legitimate?'

'By the assurance of the third affidavit, signed and attested.

This in turn is backed up by a fourth, and that by a fifth – I have here four hundred such affidavits, your honour.'

'How is the last one proven?'

'By the rider attached to the document you're holding, your honour, and witnessed by the first set of signatures. It's a proof cycle, a self-supporting system.'

'A daisyclaim,' the judge nodded. 'Very well.' He placed the paper aside. 'Mr Gaffer, the focus of this trial seems to have shifted to this fellow Mr Juno, but since I am born to serve you absolutely, that's just fine. Your attack upon the Mayor also passes me by entirely, for reasons the powerless public shall never know. You are, truly, a lovely man.'

'Thank you, your honour.'

The drylord addressed the rack of mint-eyed jury heads. 'Your big and only chance has arrived.'

The spokeshead parted a beak like a cabbage rib. 'If a mind can truly teem with one idea, we have led a rich inner life, and thank you.'

Three of the heads in the back row began screaming in a way reserved for those who needn't take a breath. It was the sound of a patriot who has given all and then seen where it went.

The head speaker continued as though prerecorded, its eyes like medals. 'The defendant is composed of litter which death will clear from him.' And the head began to emit a high whistling noise, which continued seamlessly until the court realised that the verdict had been given in full.

Satisfied, the drylord ordered Gregor to stand up, and addressed him.

'In my budding youth, the merest formality could excite me. I'm beyond the age when due process can afford me any pleasure. But today your death comes highly recommended, and so it seems your attempt to poison me at the start of this trial has returned with new alliances. Your misshapen head and lack of real direction in life mark you out as a colossal threat to our institutions, to lovely bright flowers, and even some of the better class of insect about the place. Butterflies, yes.'

'How long do we have to listen to this mattress?' Gregor hissed to De'ath, a whisper which the fluted walls amplified to an oceanic crash.

'Staring our society's etiquette in the face,' the judge continued savagely, 'point-blank and silent, without meaning or comment, offering no alternative, no critique – merely the sight of your spectacular transgression upon the very ramparts of authority. Your mania for statues – yes, mania – is thoroughly irresponsible. And so, revenge is ours. Do you wish to make a statement before you are conveyed from this place to the mime tent? Be mindful that, as a convicted felon, anything you say will appear on your permanent record.'

'There it is,' Gregor thought, and was on the stand, feeling released, strangely super-confident, well disposed toward everybody, drawing a lungful. 'Well, I made it. I never thought I'd achieve anything permanent in my life. The judge is right on the money about my depravity and lack of any constructive suggestions. I don't have a clue what's going on, and I really don't care. So I'm grateful to everyone here – especially my friends Barny, Edgy, Henrietta, pudd'n head Dumbar over there, and good old Fang, resurrected by popular demand, ha ha. I love 'em all. Even the jury of pulseless pulses here, look at 'em – top-drawer assessors of guilt, every one of 'em. More power to their cool botanical brains. Here I am, condemned, and they haven't guessed half of what I'm capable of. Beautiful. And the lawyers. Tell them you're gunna destroy the requirement for flames and they'll lick their pencils and take it down. The professionalism of those guys. I feel loose and happy. Justice is done. Everything is easy. The system works.' Gregor looked out upon the attentive courtroom. He seemed to tremble on the verge of tears. 'You know, when Edgy and I ventured into the swamps on a quest for knowledge the other day, we met the wise old hag Feral Beryl. I had doubted how useful some broken-down failure could be to anyone, but immediately the light of knowledge in her eyes pinned me. I put to her my deepest questions regarding ambition, pillow sprats, yearning, and all my mad dealings with this world. Would I wind up as I suspected, corralled at night by normally gentle neighbours and butchered wordlessly on a football field? Well, the old crone thoughtfully appraised the condition of my arse, gazed at the smoky trace of the trees against the night sky, nodded her head thoughtfully, and looked me in the eye. And she imparted this knowledge; "Always eat a fish head first. You never know." ' Gregor paused for effect. The entire court was hushed except for a couple of chefs who seemed to be experiencing some agitation. 'Was she right, or was she right? So, ladies and gentlemen, I bear you no ill-will. This is simply the end time of a keg-shaped, clueless joke with a brain the size of a Subutteo figure. Good people, when you've seen the mere door of the matter, begin to retreat, and don't make the mistake I made. Farewell – forever.'

It was soon clear to Gregor that his self-memorial had gone awry. The court had become humbled. The jury heads were squitting some silver spores which for them were tears. The public spectators too were feeling pity and regret like it was going out of style. 'Your honour,' said the head speaker, 'we wish to acquit.'

'No – not acquit, not acquit!' Gregor shouted.

'I agree,' said the judge. 'The accused is free to go, and all trace of these proceedings are hereby struck from the record.'

'The record?' Gregor shrieked. 'But it's permanent! Permanent! I'm guilty! I've done it all! No alibi! I'm a monster! When I see a nice person I slice his gizzard as a matter of routine! Nap chickens!' Gregor leapt from the stand, blurting his every imagining in a spasm of panicked candour. He snatched the affidavit from the judge's desk and scrunched it under Gaffer's nose. 'I'm taking this home to Mr Belly!' he shrieked, and stuffed it into his own mouth, chewing as he grabbed one of the jury heads and banana-kicked it into the spectators' gallery amid screams. 'I'm doing it! I'm doing it! Take it or leave it!'

'What's this disgrace?' the judge was shouting as Gregor ran past the podium.

Gregor stood peeing in the corner and bellowed at the rafters, 'Good news! I'm learning! I'm learning!' The pasta wall began to soften and sag, wilting open and slapping to the floor. Part of the roof shuddered and tilted with a bang, flour sifting down. The courthouse began crumbling. The judge's podium dissolved like a honeycomb candle. Screaming idiots were trying to run, skidding across the slimy floor. Splinters of pasta were flying like detonated glass.

'I'm bored,' said BB Henrietta.

'I feel terrible,' said Barny. 'Let's go – you coming, Edgy?'

'Not yet – the Mayor might say something else.'

Barny and BB wandered out through a hole in the wall just before the pasta lattice roof fell in and hit the floor like custard.

9

Hex Enduction Hour

Nature can get away with anything

Barny slept so deeply he had to grow up every morning, and perhaps the day never held enough time for him to reach full adulthood. This night he dreamt again of the razor larynx shooting from the sea, its eyes black flukes without detail, a mouth like a downturned horseshoe – and his own fear sent him running again, away from Chloe and the shore, to Beltane Carom's garden. In fact the yard configuration formed a wall behind Carom, as though he were floating on his back above it. Angels sharp as knives darted around him. 'Logic is only another garden,' Carom said. 'Anything in life can serve as a doorway to understanding – some open straight on to it, while others open on to a long corridor full of stinking garbage. Shove imagination to join your rent, and it becomes something else.'

Barny's disinterest was mild and amiable, without obstinacy. 'I still don't get it, ma'am.'

'The truth drinks last, when everyone's gone home. That tin homunculus for instance – the most strangely detailed things are done as a diversion. The Powderhouse, the Church of Automata – the same theology begins them all.'

'What do you mean.'

'Dangers of clarity.'

'That doesn't seem much of a danger at the moment. This

is exactly the way you talk in real life – why do you have to be doing this in a dream?'

'I'm being watched,' the shaman whispered, and Barny found himself watching Prancer Diego leave the snout distillery. Diego once left the house with a demon on his back and, thinking it was a duffel bag, stuffed a football down its throat. Now he spotted Barny and frolicked over, dispensing insults like caramels, strumming a nerve lute, his tears flowing upward. 'Proposition one – never empty the trash. Proposition two – contort so your shadow is a key. Yes, it's me – and not a moment too soon I see. The sky fills me with feelers, their industry of mouths confidently pouching, oh I giggle, I giggle.'

Barny shoved him away and ran across the pennyground acres. Showers and wages on the land flapped.

As the sun set Bo began to soften and shine, turning to sugar. Barny entered and found Bo glistening silently on a chair, realised the time and cursed, looking at his watch. He had wanted to ask him something, it would have to wait until morning.

Barny awoke suddenly. Who the hell was Bo? He didn't know anyone called Bo. Looking aside, Barny found that BB Henrietta was asleep beside him. He was in her house and they had slept together last night after the trial. So much for fighting the nightmare. He had re-smashed the fragments of his relationship with Chloe. He was a monster.

Barny staggered through the dark into the bathroom. There were inexplicable containers everywhere. 'Body gel,' he read from a label. He found a hand mirror and placed it on the floor facing upward. What were those weird words the shaman had spoken to summon his demon ally?

Before Barny had done anything the mirror began to ring and Rakeman emerged as creepy as a chirp from a breakfast egg. It came seething into shape and stood there. The air trickled slowly around it.

'This is the worst night of my life,' said Barny. There he was having fun at a friend's trial, and the next thing he knew he was in a cramped bathroom with a tragic-looking creature made entirely of ankles.

Rakeman blew ashes and other shite out of a mouth like a sack. The electric sockets were bleeding.

'Are you using my toothbrush?' asked BB Henrietta, appearing naked in the doorway. She registered the etiolated saw doctor fluctuating in blasts of spinelight, shook her head, turned and left.

Barny kicked the mirror and it skitted across the floor, hitting the closing door. It flipped over, blinking the demon from view, and Barny stamped on it, the glass crunching like a key in a lock.

He staggered panting into the bedroom. BB Henrietta was pulling on her jeans and generally tearing about the place. 'Draft log or not,' she said, 'that's the last time I ever have sex with you.'

His sanity long abandoned as an impossible dream, doomed Eddie Gallo didn't have any serious reservations about giving hospitality to a creature which appeared to have a diamond hammer for a head. He opened his cottage door and smiled a friend straight away. 'Good morning to you. As Bingo Violaine said, "Never learn a saying from behind a door – mishearing could lead to embarrassment." Come in.'

'My name is Dietrich Hammerwire – I have followed your opposition campaign with interest, doomed Eddie Gallo.' He looked around the living room. 'Spring onions in a vase, eh?'

Gallo called from the kitchen. 'And jars with bonnets.'

'There's a tortoise in the drinks cabinet.'

'I know – heck of a deal isn't it? You'll have to excuse these elaborate trousers. Today's a colonic holiday for my people.'

'It's these tiny cribs that scare me.'

'Just a hobby – made from fishbone.'

'I notice so much more these days. I see your hair has grown to resemble a cardigan.' Dietrich jabbed a claw at Gallo's forehead. 'I'm new here. What's this?'

'The forehead is the head's palm. Not from Accomplice? How is that?'

'Do you know what hell is, doomed Eddie Gallo?'

'Not much. Bit of a tense atmosphere round there I expect. Lot of awkward silences and that sort of thing. You say you've followed m'campaign for Mayor? Seen the new angle?' He presented Dietrich with a poster.

'"Understand My Legs" is not a campaign slogan.'

'Know the legs, the rest will follow. Biscuit?'

'Thank you. And what's this rubbish about you sensing a flower?'

Gallo looked on without comprehension.

'Do you understand, doomed Eddie Gallo, that you will never be Mayor as long as you continue this way?'

'Oh, I'm fine – though I've been treated like a woolly monkey, I'm determined to remain bright no matter what.'

'I find your optimism positively morbid, doomed Eddie Gallo. I . . .'

Learning from the Powderhouse's strutting procedures, doomed Eddie Gallo had established a personal regimen of quantum shrugging – he would allow all he didn't know or understand to accumulate for several days and, at saturation point, shuck his shoulders hundreds of times in quick succession. Those who witnessed this would think he was having a fit, though he usually continued speaking quite clearly during the procedure. As he began to shudder before Dietrich Hammerwire, he was baffled at the creature's sudden startled stare and backwards retreat to the door. 'Thanks for visiting,' he called as Dietrich's face withdrew and the door closed.

Later he was watering the front garden and a truck hauled up, steam pouring out of it. After topping up the radiator in a neighbourly way, he had a chat with the driver, who appeared to be a small artificial girl made of plastic and cardboard. She seemed very interested in his policy ideas and they drove out to the flyover stump on the north edge of town. They sat near the cliff edge and opened a packed lunch of bananas and digestive biscuits. Gallo pointed to a heave of concrete waves, severed steel reinforcement shafts poking out at the breaklines. 'The sloths did that – they explode when accosted, and every attempt to vault this canyon blasted more off the road until, well, you can see – it's no more than a ramp now. I plan to bring timber from the Awkward Forest and extend it.' Gallo indicated some hard-pan. 'That used to be called a lay-by. It was purely for sex.' They walked to the very edge. A wooden sign was coughing in the updraft. Gallo handed her the binoculars and she clicked them against the glass of her eyes. The opposite side of the canyon was heatwarping, patched here and there with vegetation and shot through with black sheets of rock. She swept the glasses along the far ridge. It seemed desolate. There were no people. 'Look down there,' Gallo suggested. She peered through the binoculars at the canyon floor, which was a lost world of mist and vegetation, speckled here and there with white dots. 'Those are manuscripts,' Gallo told her, and gestured over at the offices of Nimble Champ Books, the rear of which projected over the abyss. 'Convenient. There's a few phantoms down there too but they're rubbish, frankly. Useless to man and beast.'

Gallo began talking about the Miasma and Amy's play, how he planned to bake hundreds of pies made of pure lard. He soon forgot that the doll was there, and started chirping like a bird, chuckling at his own amusements. He had zoned out completely when Maquette told him she was interested in the play. 'Especially if there are animals.'

'I'm sure there'll be a part in it for you,' said doomed Eddie Gallo. 'We are all one community.'

The truck, this time, was dead. They would have to drop by Abblatia's and steal another one.

Mayor Rudloe plucked up the phone. 'Ah, Grand Dollimo – how are you and your waxen atrocities this morning? The escaped doll? Yours is it? I'm sorry, I do not assign rights to novelties.' He paused, then his voice was jerky and high.

'Max Gaffer paid you a visit? Without my sanction, I assure you. No, he doesn't know you provide the Gubba Men. He knows nothing of our arrangement, he shouldn't have approached you. The Steinways? Now don't do anything rash. I've a beef to pick with that shyster myself. Keep those monsters under lock and key, I'll deal with this. I assure you I am appalled by his acts. He will be dismissed as soon as his career is over. Goodbye.'

It was perfectly clear to Rudloe that he would not be seeing Gaffer again except as a deadly foe or other inconvenience. Stung into action by the lawyer's betrayal, he looked fiercely at a corner of the desk. 'I'm ready for anything,' he barked at the empty room, at which a dab of demon lengthened to the floor, walking on. 'Well, menace me quickly or not at all, I've matters to attend to.' But Dietrich Hammerwire seated himself opposite and asked for a job. The Mayor was tortuously aghast. 'You think I'll employ any out-at-elbows fiend who walks in here? Straight out of purgatory and leaning in the crackers?'

'There's no point in concealing my preference,' said Dietrich mildly, the fresh dawn light glinting off his hell-blasted cowling. He gazed outside – there was a man standing atop a high stepladder in the Square and consulting a book. Children surrounded the scene. 'What's that moron doing?'

'Learning braille, apparently,' the Mayor muttered. He was wary, knowing that a deal with a demon invariably entailed a number of hair-raising provisos. 'How do I know you're not a placeman for the forces of hell?

'Oh, give it a year and then take a view on it.'

'So what's your advice for a kick-off?'

'Put on a dress and kill everyone you see.'

'A dress? Kill?

'Is there any reason why we can't begin immediately?'

'Aren't you the bastard who disguised yourself as a normal fella to convince me I should win over the masses by pushing a servant off the balcony?'

'Sounds like the sort of thing I would suggest.'

'Exactly. And now it's dresses and immediate killing.'

'Just so. What do the people have on you?'

'They know me because the van sings my name. Blame the sentry for the scarce attacks.'

'You might try a more folksy role in the Miasma proceedings, perhaps. Good sport and man of the people. Then confound all by saying something interesting as the eclipse occurs.'

'Interesting, eh?' Rudloe turned the notion over in his head.

'You could even try apology.'

'It's true – that apology gag gets 'em every time.'

'It has the element of surprise, and a fairly long rhetoric decay rate.' Dietrich seemed bored, distracted – it was all too easy. 'There's the philosophy of politics, and there's the career of politics – the two are not good for each other. Where the two meet, the process and machinery of politics is excreted. That's why you're full of shit, Mayor.'

'Well the fact remains I'm the big wheel around here. I'll consider your application. Leave me now – oh and excuse all these megabugs.'

'Have you tried paraffin?'

'Yes.'

'Have you tried honesty?'

'You're joking, of course.'

When the anvil-headed demon was gone, Rudloe put a call through to the Conglomerate.

10

Spigot Girl

It's only good manners to wave to one's assassin

Mike Abblatia was a blot of pain which increased with each vehicle he lost. When the plastic child roared away in a truck, he had felt his back expand, small bones creaking. Doctor Perfect had a real knack for removing important meat but Abblatia approached his surgery as though it were a narrowing corner of hope. 'Enter my empire of emergencies,' called the Doctor. 'I was just carving the image of a screaming leper into this old root beam.' And he tapped the leper's nose. 'Wasn't I, matey? Now – Mike Abblatia isn't it? Don't see you often – keep yourself to yourself, eh? Well, don't worry. Things have moved on a little since we tied one end of a rope to the patient's tonsils and the other end to a rampaging horse. Sit up on this crushed car.'

There were two cars with flattened roofs – the other one was occupied by what appeared to be a large smashed fungus. Abblatia sat on the free surface.

Doctor Perfect took up a pair of tongs and began tugging at Abblatia's ears. 'These legs of yours have seen better days – if they are legs. Been kicking badgers, have we? And your nostrils appear to have a life of their own. Look up to the corner. Now to the other corner. See those things that look like pancakes? They're a kind of mould growing up there. It gives me hope that life can thrive in the grimmest places. Give a sort of cough which is loaded with significance, will you? Good. And again? I understand.' He tossed the hammer aside. 'Well, I'm afraid your brain has lain fallow for some years, your torso is completely uninteresting and your balls are a mystery. I could offer you a phial of goatwater but you would refuse it, chundering like billy-o. I'm at a loss as to what you expect of me.'

'My back's the problem, Doctor.'

'Bit dicey, is it? Alright, take off this shapeless garment and lay on your front.'

After laying forward amid silence a while, Abblatia heard the Doctor pronounce. 'This "back" as you charmingly characterise it – you're aware that if it was any more swollen I should have to perform a citizen's arrest? Been having a lot of fun with it haven't you? However, the good news is, I can help you with knives. Lie still, laddie.'

Abblatia felt a cold tingling down his spine.

'I'm cutting the seam. There's no blood. Pushing the edges aside. It's completely clean. A sort of damp fuzz in there. Seems to be some kind of fibrous mush, like the white innards of a seedy loaf.'

Mike Abblatia's attention was wandering, his eyes floating over the walls of coloured hux tinctures and flay charts. His attention drifted to the other car and he recognised it as one which had been stolen from him two years before. The one he lay upon, he realised, had been boosted slightly more recently.

'Fascinating,' the Doctor was saying.

Abblatia sat up as though tranced, and pulled his shirt on.

The Doctor seemed fazed by his patient's capacity for autonomous will during the examination. 'Off somewhere, are we laddie?'

Mike Abblatia walked out through the time lounge and up the muddy slope, opening the rotten hatch into the alley as sunlight exploded upon him.

*

The Conglomerate had sent for Max Gaffer and he entered the flesh basement prepared to adopt explanation demeanour. Hanging alimentary loops dragged across his face.

'Here he comes,' said one of the voices from the half-light, 'his authority in one hand and his broken heart in the other. Beware turning the truffle of *that* one's brain.'

'We've heard about your obscure debacle in the courtroom.'

'Oh I see.' Gaffer knew this was a failure, pure and simple. By the time the courthouse had sagged completely, the judge was able only to purse his lips in a funny way – or perhaps he was simply inclined to do so. According to procedure the jury heads were tossed on a bonfire and the judge was sent to the dryhouse, a small unfurnished bungalow on the edge of town. Like many drylords before him, he would stand silent in that dim concrete-floored room as night turned to day and day turned to night, crumbling slowly to a heap resembling powdered braken. 'You approved my advancement.'

'Guilt and implication. As last-ditch as a spring-snake in a failure's mouth. You went beyond your remit. The Mayor serves us well, knowingly or not. So, etherically you outrank him. It also means you're no longer quite anchored here. Unlike the Mayor, who's dug in like the true bastard.'

Gaffer stumbled over slimy bones, grasping for balance at hanging rinds of gut. 'What do you mean?

'The Mayor's corruption is dependable. You? You're ambitious – and dealing with poisons more instant than ours. It makes you rather too volatile, useful only for the very short term.'

'I'll make amends, anything. Give me a contract, I'll sign in colour.'

The voices came thick and fast from different parts of the organ reef.

'The idea has merit, as trash.'

'Treasonable dealings are forgiven only when successful.'

'You're as duped as a battle surgeon – a hack.'

'But why open that can of nerves.'

'You entertain us with harm, merely.'

'Give our regards to your gigantic host.'

'Death occurs here, my friend. On your neck.'

Amid the sense of nerve bodies heaving, Gaffer felt a yank at his throat and he came loose, hitting a hard corner of the room. Such gentlemen always needed cold stone, even if they didn't have food. Gaffer gagged at the aroma of hamburgers frying in the skull. Another barb dug into his side and a film of milky colour clouded his eyes. 'Ah, the moment of the face falling apart, spattered with angel,' said one of the mouths. But Gaffer had gotten turned around. He was on the step out of here – he tried to stand, nudging at the doors.

'D'you mind telling me what you're doing?' came the commanding shout from behind as he crawled through the doors into the silverine foyer. Far away was the elevator door. He glimpsed strange dry flowers, and then blood pooling on the carpet under him. Opening his shirt, he let it flow down to the metal barb at his chest, which seemed to soak it up some, though the beak made a noise like a screaming infant.

Gaffer climbed the spiral stairs to his oval bonehouse, throwing himself inside and collapsing in an armchair. His wound had begun to clot a little. The Grand Dollimo was at the corner bar, fixing a mazarinade. 'You really had no idea of the nature of my arrangement with the Mayor.'

'How did you get in here.'

'And the match girl, our runaway – no result. Yet all the while, you claimed to have the Mayor's blessing.'

'That statement was only local – in fact it did not persist beyond the room.'

Dollimo's waxen hatchet man advanced through a doorway, its earth-red skin blazing in strips of sunlight.

'Had you telephoned,' Gaffer breathed, half-rising out of

the chair, 'I could have saved you an inconvenient journey. I'll not concede to be slaughtered today.'

'In the coffin we return to the wild.' The Dollimo approached Gaffer with two glasses, handing him one. Gaffer sank down again. 'We blot there and sag. Plenty of time to relax our stance when the time comes. Until then.' And the Dollimo raised his drink in salutation. He did not join Gaffer in drinking – his glass mask made this impossible. He strolled to one of the broad windows, which showed a far strip of blue ocean. 'Do you know that human beings used to do the work of the Gubba Men? They were replaced, finally, with our blandflesh.'

Gaffer played for time, eyeing the room for a weapon. 'Why do it that way? Why the Gubba Men?'

'Something to do with dissonance. Human beings acting less than human, and thus being treated as such, yet acting surprised or offended when it happened. This way, however, all accords with itself – and no feelings to be hurt. I thought you would have guessed that Distaff Plastique here is an advanced Gubba unit. No feeling, you see. His core temperature's way below zero, like a tailor. Distaff is empty life, a tool made for one job.'

As Distaff neared him, Gaffer saw that the automaton held the Iron Smile in its vinyl hand. He smashed his glass and launched himself at Distaff, slashing the slick upholstery of its forehead. The sentinel knocked him aside with an easy swipe of its arm.

The Grand Dollimo was chuckling softly to himself. 'That red pepper brain of his showing through like sofa leather? A class act all the way, isn't he? Distaff is a future without content – your future.'

'I'll find your doll,' Gaffer barked as Distaff Plastique locked a hand on his shoulder, preventing him from rising.

'The doll knows nothing. D'you think it's that easy? Place a brain cell in a jointed doll and bingo? D'you think the dolls, those totems, all this mechanical business, is what it's about? What makes more noise than the death of a man? The death of a secret.'

The Iron Smile was a dull beaten half-mask rattling with attachments.

'What secret. What are the dolls and all hiding?'

'That we can never be creation's original stem, perhaps?'

Distaff placed the dented metal bridle over Gaffer's mouth.

'I don't believe it,' said Gaffer. 'You lashed together some sort of religion out of smoked glass and chicken wire, why?'

Distaff tightened the first screw with an automatic screwdriver – it went through Gaffer's face and into his cheekbone.

'What's it all about? To hide what?'

The thinner bones snapped audibly as five more screws screamed into Gaffer's skull, locking the mask to his face. His features were pinned in place.

The Dollimo leaned down at him. 'Happy?'

Gaffer couldn't help but smile.

He groped down the twelve steps to Sweeney's cavern.

Enthroned in a veined hull, the white shell emperor floated his head around. 'Ah, war returned from exotic climes, overloud for the home. Report, report, as florid as you can.'

Nerve guylines twanged as the Ruby Aspict descended from the sky-high roof. Gaffer crawled across freezing sickstone, puzzle-toothed and broken. 'Barny . . . appears to be kept aloft by efforts invisible and constant as hummingbird wings.'

'Nice touch. Continue.'

'He's happy to care for the winged and stepping animals of the earth.'

'Happiness sounds rather dull.'

'Maybe it's the way I describe it. Then again, maybe not. Glee, at least, is worth the effort.'

'Glee? Sounds like a jelly preserve.'

'Well,' breathed Gaffer, at a loss, 'life continues – the primeval soup prevails.'

'Black mud is no consolation, I'm afraid. Still, many a slip between pup and tip. And the eclipse approaches, oiling the skylight. However, since agreeing to put your few remaining principles beyond use, you've exhausted m'patience with petty and somewhat lurid reprisals. What are your personal intrigues? A spark in the grandeur of my life. Wipe that smile off your face, man.'

'I'm ashamed, your majesty,' burbled the crouching figure as the roiling red Aspict settled behind him.

'You clearly thought hell was cosmetic, fangs sewn into your jacket and so forth. Personality retention. No such luck, regrettably. Time for you to graduate.'

Cold voltage branched through the lawyer and his anatomy became an open secret, flents of skin flying like sawdust. The black of his suit became a thickness of constantly roiling spiders, his own bleached ribs replaced the white of his shirt, and twelve sleek swords sprang erect from his skull, each leaking a slow excess of toxins which ran in a constant tide down his shiny grinning face. His eyes were glints the size of nail parings.

His reflection tumbled in the turning Aspict. Relieved that he would still be able to pass himself off in the legal community, he turned to Sweeney and bowed low his towering crown of bayonets. 'You do me too much honour sir. Life, merely – a dainty loss. May I realise all is dross.'

'The demon Maximillion,' Sweeney pronounced with satisfaction. 'Charmed.'

11

The Gale

*Like a cyclist, the critic is assuming you'll get
out of the way*

Despair is not a subtle business. Barny entered the town's
celebration of culture with his lion loping beside him. Scardummy Garden was filled with goofy project action, skriking
kids, busted porphyry columns, erratic behaviour, eyes filming over, cameras from the Douglas Bar Show, carnage, and
one trotting dog. All the town's statues stood planted in
earth, some decked and maintained, some left to the flowers.
To Barny everything passed in mourning.

Edgy had stolen a truck from Mike Abblatia and filled it
with glass harpy pies – this had collided with a truck which
doomed Eddie Gallo had stolen from Mike Abblatia and
filled with lard pies. The wares had become a little mixed as
they scrabbled to reload, but who would know or care about
anything either of these idiots thought or tried to do? Barny
wandered up to doomed Eddie Gallo's stall and noticed a
strange mechanical doll playing under the table. 'What's
this, doomed Eddie Gallo?'

'A doll,' said doomed Eddie Gallo, giving Barny a compli-
mentary pie. 'A sort of talking mask, really. Escaped from
that silent temple of needles on the corner of town.'

'Who's pulling her strings?'

'No crank organ for this glass-eyed beauty, Barny. She's
cut her own umbilical. I like her.' And Gallo began shouting
his pie pitch to the crowd, scaring everyone. 'Pies! Perhaps

you should consider other things a waste of time? Pies! Perhaps you should consider other things a waste of time? Pies!'

At his nearby stall, Edgy realised that this pie tirade would work to his own advantage also, and began moving his mouth as though he were forming the words himself. 'I am the shining man,' he thought.

The lion bellied under Gallo's table to follow the capering doll, and Barny went behind the stall to find them sat together on the grass. He joined them beneath the whiskery trees, and offered the doll a piece of pie.

'I eat carpets,' she said.

Barny thought about it for a while, drawing a blank.

A fairy-like dragonfly landed on the grubby pink prosthetic plastic of her arm. She watched it until it took off again.

Nearby was a struggle-statue of a man tangled with a sort of mechanical mosquito the size of a sewing machine. The bug's rusty legs were caught in the statue as though in resin. The whole thing looked finished and ditched, unlike the other figures here. 'Silence,' said Barny. 'It's going to be silence from now on for me.'

'I like this furry,' said the doll, putting her hand into the deep fur of Mister Braintree. The lion licked his chops and gave a snaggled yawn.

'He's my friend,' Barny told her. 'His purring is twenty times the volume of a household cat. He can jump as far as forty feet and as high as fifteen feet.'

Maquette rested on the lion's head. Barny looked toward the fair's centre – everything seemed to be slowing, GI Bill's stride swimming to an almost stop, gaps opening in the pressure-world as the Mayor tortuously ascended a pyramid of dead tailors, a sluggish blue balloon passing him.

The Mayor tottered a little and used the mike stand to find his balance. He surveyed the crowd and turned to the demon Dietrich. 'Present yourself like a theme park and the louts appear.'

'The mike's open, Mayor.'

'God almighty. Well everyone, here we are in the Dummy Precinct. Nothing like a hard and ringleted head to make a fella look classical. Tedious grass around here and so on, you'll notice. But we won't let that distract us from this foolhardy escapade, yes, these grotesque antics, many of which are already looking to me like a relic from the past. This day will melt away, and so will you. But until that time, there will be no respite from entertainment – it will be brutal. I cannot overemphasise the dangers inherent in this nonsense. Give yourselves up to drunkenness and wild conjecture. Evade, evade, evade as factory funnels pump stains into the sky. You are all my children. I feel the rest of the introduction is rubbish, I'll let you imagine it.' The Mayor began to mime atrociously, losing the attention of his audience in seconds.

'Democracy is the right to add to the swarm's thrum or to remain silent.'

'The mike's still open, Mayor.'

'Oh, hell – well everyone, to begin the Miasma, I now unveil a portrait of myself, rendered by the esteemed Undo Cakewalk. You have my authority to understand the thing.' He pulled on a string and the veil fell from a picture stand. The painting seemed to portray a furtive herring aiming a mallet at a shivering dog, the entire scene heavy with fog and darkness.

'It's a picture of a decomposing camel,' came an appalled voice from the crowd.

'Why?' wailed another. 'Why show us this?'

'Er, I declare the Miasma of Culture, open,' the Mayor stammered, and stepped down from the pyramid as the band struck up a warning, thought consultants decamped in panic and a gout of smilers looked with hidden despair upon kids riffling their gills like new playing cards. The Mayor surveyed the scene. 'Maybe it's better this way,' he said mournfully. In his new role as adviser to the Mayor, Dietrich had convinced him to play a part in BB's theatrical production, something Rudloe barely understood. The demon slapped him on the back, directing him toward the makeshift stage, and followed him, looking to the sky.

Along the main arcade were stalls of caged boneseed stretched with tailorskin, selling umbilical soda and feather-aerial radios. Mr De'ath operated a children's puppet show or so-called 'campaign of terror', presenting his version of 'The Tell-Tale Heart' in which the protagonist buried a strawberry under the floor and was haunted by a lack of ideas. Flesh performers experimented with cheek holes and new ragged mouths. There was a 'honking booth' where a man foretold futures of violent death and failure. Entitled 'Horrifying Futures', it sent a few people scurrying and, once the word was out, attracted no more.

Fang presented an exhibit called 'Do Glass Chairs Make You Uncertain?' Citizens were urged to sit in some glass chairs and see how they felt. Rooster showcased his 'lard music' – 'He croon jowly and unsolvable' went the publicity. His tone was in fact unusually surly, on the edge of trucu-lence, as he strutted with a barely-restrained violence. He folded a cloth napkin during his rendition of 'Every Single Time', then presented it for view with a sharp, threatening flourish. There in the funnel were collected houseflies.

Prancer Diego wrapped himself in sack and chains and, struggling for what would be recorded subsequently as a full three days, chided his furious onlookers for lacking the 'precious gift of patience'.

'Tight show, Prancer,' Edgy called during the first tense hour.

Prancer was distracted, ungrateful. 'Mark me up for sev-enty courses of lashing with a hurlypen whip, target me, target me!'

Gregor did a strange 'mirror duet' with an empty frame, on the other side of which stood his statue. It was inappro-priately romantic and he began snogging his image, climbing it with hugging legs. This tidy little spectacle revolted one and all, including his girlfriend Magenta Blaze. She punched the nose of his statue, breaking Gregor's nose and her own.

The guy in the honking booth up and died. The lucky dip was a predictably violent affair. The Captain reproached everyone for their groaning and there was a nasty scene. Here was a stall selling books written in nondescript, the language of walking death. And in balance near the pie stalls stood Crash Test Nureyev's exhibit devoted to Bingo Violaine, copies of *Puff-Adder Christmas*, *Conker Fight My Arse* and *Hand It To Sparky* laid out for sale. Nureyev constantly pounded his forehead with the heels of his palms and repeated details of the author's life. 'Wrote books. Big ones with an oil brush. His manner lodged icicles in guests. Acted grandly offended. He was drummed out of his body years ago. Violaine rests in peace – the world rests in igorance. You think learning's boring? History's no virgin.' And so on, until Barny, watching ants in the grass nearby, had learnt all he could about the armoured dots.

'Those are just great,' he smiled, chuffed, and stood up. 'Now let's go see BB's play.' Maquette and the lion stood to go with him. Finding the stage area, Barny sat on the outer edge of the seating. Doomed Eddie Gallo fetched the doll to be costumed as a lion for her appearance on stage. Mister Braintree stretched out on the pattern of green and green leaves. Barny noticed Chloe was among the crowd, her white face open to the show.

Behind the stage Mayor Rudloe had entered dressmaker bedlam. BB Henrietta pushed him through the throng. 'You sicken me, Mayor, but that pet demon of yours says you'll give me a lotta money for this – stand over there.'

'Me? Offer you money? I doubt that.'

'We'll fill any faults with music. Tentative, halting affection is something the band can play. Sometimes they stop completely. I said stand over there mister. This is the bloke I was warning you about, everyone. He'll be playing the monster in Barny's nightmare.'

Rudloe looked about him, nervous. 'I peddle twelve expressions, all disapproving.'

The dressing tent was packed with freaks. Barny was being

played by GI Bill, who in regard to intelligence considered himself at least the equal of a twig. He viewed Rudloe with open hostility. 'He no act. No light on him.'

'Don't we have any costumes? Great plays glow in the dark, don't they?'

'Not this one,' said Amy Gort, clicking herself into a harness. 'This is a work of the New Truculence. There's the script.'

Rudloe leafed through it. '"The bear *entrez*" – what the hell?'

'Let's hope it goes better than last year's production,' said Baz McCaffrey, a dedicated actor. 'I had to physically attack the audience, in a brutal violation of my training.'

'Remember, people – tickle their standards with a plague of imagination.' BB clapped her hands. 'While away the narrative in noise and alarm. And never say an audience is unappreciative – just say the play was meant for people with lower expectations. Let's go.'

The Mayor looked out through the curtains and spotted a lion in the audience. 'Yellow nerves bunched into the shape of a lion!'

'It's a lion, you idiot!' snapped BB Henrietta as Amy Gort was winched into the eaves. 'Get out there!' And she pushed him on to the stage.

'A monster!' bellowed GI Bill, climbing into bed and pointing at the Mayor. He pronounced the more complex lines with infinite care. 'Observe! Now its mouth distends, oozing blood. Here in the lopsided chicken coop of my house, on the slope of the landing, a carnivore of unusual design does stand.'

'It's the Mayor!' someone shouted from the audience.

'He's being haunted by the Mayor!'

A shabby lion pounced onstage and Rudloe screamed like a woman, getting a few laughs. As he realised it was a sinister automaton in a suit the scene changed around him and BB shoved him offstage – the principal actors were now seated in a crappy replica of Snorters cafe. BB played Gregor by filling her cheeks with air when she wasn't required to talk, signifying fatness. Doomed Eddie Gallo was strolling through the part of Edgy. 'Well, er, Bubba,' he said to GI Bill, 'this monster sounds about as real as my arse.'

'Your arse isn't real?'

The cast paused for a big laugh from the audience, but heard only the fizz of a few flies.

'When I consider the miracle of centipedes and their bodily needs,' said GI Bill haltingly, 'I disturb myself upwards, above normal concerns. Already bedposts are mere details, soon the rest will follow. Just from thinking about centipedes.'

'Well you're disturbing everyone else too, Bubba. Just because you saw some jangly fiend in the window.'

'So regret me.'

'Let's go to the Dummy Garden,' said BB Henrietta, 'because I love my statue, if you know what I mean.'

In the garden set, they stood with the undead Fang. Behind them, BB rolled around on a giant potato. The entire scene had about it an atmosphere of futile despondency. 'It's no good, Barny,' said Fang to GI Bill. 'Gregor's too fat, Edgy's too thin, you're an idiot, and here we are with these statues. And like these statues, when I die I shall be planted in soil, ugly worms trying my patience.' And Fang turned, stepping off the stage and dropping head first into the audience. One of his arms lay twitching behind the footlights.

'Chloe is gone,' said GI Bill, absently picking up the arm. 'But we're boys, and we don't care.' And the representations of Barny, Edgy and Gregor began dancing mischievously.

Baz McCaffrey sprang into view, wearing Edgy's candelabra and capering like an imp. 'Beltane Carom here – look upon this mirror, and be helped by demons.'

The three lads swore allegiance, saluting, and declared in unison, 'We will remember.'

In a blast of smoke, Baz was gone.

The court scene tried for gravitas. Sags Dumbar, his translucent cuttlebone skull at odds with the ease and pleasure of the audience, played the judge. Edgy had escaped his stall long enough to play the lawyer Max Gaffer, and swept back and forth in a black cape, berating BB Henrietta. 'Look over there at Mr Juno. This twitching lunatic's parents are actually garments of some kind.'

'Are you sure.'

'They look very like garments, that's what I mean.'

'You should say what you mean then.'

'Oh really? And what did you mean when you,' and Edgy pretended to look at a document, though he actually scrutinised the forehead of an Alsatian which had wandered onstage, ' "smashed everything you could see?" '

'I was passing so I thought I'd select a lamp and break it with some stones.'

'What did you do it for?'

'For the consequences.'

'Not a good reason.'

'Well, here I am.'

'And welcome. Yes, welcome to the festival of whimsy we like to call "justice".'

'I confess, I confess!' BB contrived an expression like a stomped flower. 'I encourage everyone to engage our civic statuary in sex, sex, sex for fun and education, and why not? It's love, it's love! What else? As Bingo Violaine said, "A successful sin should make a difference, shouldn't it?" '

The audience seemed to have become a scowling contest, the aim being to include the maximum number of facial folds and involutions in that expression. During a set change Edgy delivered a dirge, sung with an air of cloak-trailing melancholy. 'Learn well, children,' he intoned in a French accent, 'the human soul will turn, like mayonnaise. Just leave it long enough in this stupid world without anything interesting going on. I pray for you.'

'The dancer has no concept of duration, does he?' remarked the Mayor backstage, and BB Henrietta slapped him eleven times around the face. 'Why?' he howled. But the next scene was beginning.

GI Bill stood amid broken furniture. 'Chloe is gone and I am the Donkey of Failure. If only someone could comfort me – can it be true?' And he looked up. At this point Amy Gort was supposed to be lowered to the stage on wires, playing a trumpet. But by this time, Amy was so drunk with the boredom of it all, she had passed out and was lowered lank as a drowned witch. The trumpet fell from her slack hand and knocked GI Bill unconscious. Doomed Eddie Gallo had to take over as Barny. 'I feel so ashamed,' he read, fumbling through the script. 'Broken up with Chloe for only three minutes, and already I have rogered half the town. But I remember the mirror and the help of demons.' He put a hand mirror face-up on the stage floor and recited a nonsensical invocation. BB Henrietta shoved Mayor Rudloe through the curtains to stand over the mirror as though magically apported. The audience could by now make no sense of the events unfolding – why was placid candidate doomed Eddie Gallo having sex with half the town and then summoning his fiercest political rival through a mirror?

The plot exited before the actors, wrote the drama critic for *The Blank Stare* during the performance. *And their contribution was a groan of green cosmetic method. We viewed their activities as a threatening commotion. Mayor Rudloe's illness swung open and roared into the crowd. Help me.*

So when a great rack of flayed bone folded up out of subspace, bringing with it air pain and blasts of sour disaster, the audience barely reacted. Mayor Rudloe was sitting on the shoulders of Rakeman amid shimmering crackles of cold electricity. 'That hopeless amateur,' Baz McCaffrey gasped from the wings.

Barny was throwing himself down the row, blurting at Chloe, 'I never called down Amy Gort on wires with a trumpet – I slept with BB Henrietta.'

'You mean that zombie was meant to be me?' As she looked up at him the air was suddenly chill. Miles of sky turned grey as a burger-sized chunk was taken out of the sun, growing into darkness. The sound of rain pelleting against cheap seats completed the scene.

The Mayor shouted, 'A staggering amount of water appears to be landing and landing for no reason on house and field alike.'

'It's raining, Mayor,' Dietrich hollered. 'And you're riding on the shoulders of Rakeman, Sweeney's help, a kind of living fence! Beware the beast, man!'

'What about Rudloe Manor? This rain of yours'll debauch the masonry.'

'Don't worry, Mayor,' Barny called. 'It's just the eclipse. Dad says it's happened before. My mum stopped calling him Julius that day and began knitting beggars out of her own veins. When she finished them and snipped them free, they would always shiver and wobble, leaving the house straight away.'

Alerted, Rakeman began stretching toward Barny like a knotted sheet, it's howl-mouth a sack of darkness. The audience bolted in several directions as the Mayor was cannonballed into the seating and left behind. The air filled with the smell of burning wires. Rakeman swerved like a train, blurring after Barny.

Rain fell like chains. Barny thought of his many happy wanderings with Chloe through these very gardens and their snort-laughing discovery of demon statues on the peripheries. He ran toward the untended edges of the precinct, the downpour tearing leaves and freaking the scene around him. There ahead, among the crab-apple trees, was a stone ladder of latticed ribs surmounted by a vortical shriek mechanism. If he destroyed this, the creature would die. But the principles of statucide would mean he himself would also be destroyed. He reached the twisted statue, and on the lawn behind him appeared the white shrike, lit by lightning, rain glistering down its bloodless wound of a head. It launched itself at Barny, twisting in mid-air and smashing into its own statue, the femur climbing frame exploding around it. Rakeman's endless throat had been cut, snow flying out of the wound. Then the demon evaporated with its replica.

The creature had tripped on something – a small new figure.

Barny returned without hurry to the seating area to find that the wooden stage was filled with the anglebars of Sweeney's many legs, the crane cab of his head peering down at Scardummy Garden and its stressed visitors. 'Look at this,' the demon gloried, 'an entire set of unopened bodies!' The scene was hung with the applause of rain.

'This fellow is Sweeney, Emperor of Cold Hell,' Dietrich commented aside to the Mayor. 'He's got an auxiliary spiral face housed inside his mouth, you'll notice, and those mandibles are capable of crushing your skull like a monkey nut.'

'Skull, is that what he wants? I can't!'

Quake shrugged the sidewalks.

'What's that?'

'Just secondary warp from the creepchannel due to such an inconvenient fiend coming through.'

'You mean this one's more inconvenient than most? Don't just stand around informing me of the crucial facts, do something!'

'Dietrich Hammerwire,' said Sweeney, and hove its huge face toward the demon and the Mayor, its bloodshot muscles sliding whole yards. Several townspeople backed away, stumbling over seats. 'My proportions strike the times as massive, should I apologise?'

Dietrich stared at the titanic mantis. 'What have you been up to of late, sire?'

'Hatching hard meteors from my arse.'

Dietrich sighed, wearily offended. 'How unnecessary. You never disappoint, do you.'

'A baby scorpion gasps so? Dirty fame is hard on the new breed, I know. Head like a yard mailbox, you're right for this neighbourhood, Dieter. At last, no lies to live across to, yes?

You'll learn different if you haven't already. And how's the other runaway – Gettysburg? When's the wedding?'

Dietrich remained flint-faced. 'Tomorrow.'

Sweeney missed a beat. The rain was letting up. 'The Trim Reaper seems to be dead. I can't say I'm altogether surprised considering the trouble he had getting through. I'm priming Rammstein below.'

'He can talk a mean deed, at least.'

'Don't think he's up to it?'

'He's a bit lippy, that's all.'

'Spare me!' Rudloe interrupted, sinking to his knees and generally calling attention to himself. 'Take the child!' He pointed at Mister Braintree. 'She's disguised as a lion!' And he scampered over to the lion, grabbing its fur and getting a whirling, savage bite on the arse. 'My head!'

'Your arse, Mayor,' coughed Dietrich.

'And you consider this a suitable use of your time,' Sweeney sighed. Dietrich bowed his head, his tarnished armour dull in the half-light.

'It's alright, Mr Mayor,' said the doll Maquette, toddling over from the other direction and removing her costume. 'I'll go with the monster if it will help.'

'You all heard her,' shouted the Mayor to the assembled citizens. 'This child volunteers to go to hell in my place. Sound tactics, I think you'll agree. And let us never speak of this again.'

'Children burn out,' said Sweeney. 'Even this one, maybe. And it's Barny Juno I'm interested in, while optimal conditions prevail.'

'Who put this big insect here?' asked Barny, wandering over and indicating the king demon.

Sweeney brought his whaleskull face to bear on Barny. 'There is no pleasant way to say "I will destroy you". And now that I'm in your presence, I sense no power in you at all.' He plucked up the mirror. 'Consider yourself damned. This is the servants' entrance to my famous nerve tornado.

And for traditionalists there's a chain of underground fire-lakes.'

'Yes, ma'am.'

But as the demon turned the mirror to catch Barny's image, Barny was fading, benthic colours passing through his shape. A flicker of air and Barny was gone.

'Well,' chuffed Dietrich. 'Don't that just beat the biscuit.'

Sweeney looked at the empty space without comprehension. His oyster-white eyes blinked over, fogging and clearing as the light began to change. The eclipse was closing down. He had wasted his window – he began warping into the mirror, knots of cold lightning banging through the frame. His head angled at Dietrich. 'I'll kill you. That's a bargain.' And his skeleton collapsed through the portal, which fell to the grass.

Dietrich's wings rucked like a cabbage. 'That's too bad.'

12

A Ride on a Lion

Become yourself like a tap at last running clear

A warm southern breeze blew in and the grass flamed again with sunlight. BB Henrietta emerged from behind the stage and announced to the scattered crowd: 'We've abridged your reaction by poisoning the seats. Thank you for coming.'

The Mayor attempted to cradle his own arse. 'Dietrich, this afternoon's entertainment was costly. In fact at such a price an entire day would cost my life. What's this now?'

People were gathering around the false child.

'Some sort of civic overflow.'

The Brigade, a few Fuseheads and the red sentinel Distaff Plastique were among the crowd which had formed around Maquette, and the Mayor saw the opportunity for salvage. 'Yes everyone, I've delivered up that killer robot for y'pleasure.'

'I don't think there's quite any evidence to prove it's a killer robot, Mayor,' Dietrich remarked.

'To the praying classes, it's a cast iron bitch. Hello everyone, I seek no thanks.' Rudloe did in fact seek it where none could conceivably exist. 'More importantly, the jugular issue is resolved – that belief in a hinge baby with Fabergé guts is no match for cynical electioneering and a headstone crammed with footnotes. No offence meant to the Church of Automata, the Cannonites, or anyone else. Bad taste entails a kind of generosity. This fraud will be a complete success.'

A scream rang out as a small stone replica of Maquette came dragging across the grass toward the crowd. Barny Juno materialised around it as the effects of the harpy pie wore off. 'Look, Mr Mayor,' he said. 'It's a statue of Maquette. It's what trapped and killed the long demon that chased me.'

Conversation stirred. Many among the onlookers who had eaten glass meat, intentionally or otherwise, were trickling in and out of visibility.

'So?' Rudloe demanded. 'Juno, your brain gets smaller every time I look away – why are you wasting my time?'

'Her own statue. It means she's like us, a part of the community.'

Rudloe grimaced, struggling not to understand.

'Which is what the Miasma today is all about.'

'Alright,' the Mayor sighed inaudibly, resigning himself to the worst. He made a weak smile for the crowd. 'He misses nothing, this one. I have clearly stated that the doll is a killer robot. The implication was clearly that she is not a killer robot. In fact, I love the little imp.'

'You condemned her to hell,' said doomed Eddie Gallo.

'I'd have thought she'd relish the chance. And as for Barny Juno. We sometimes find it amusing to speak to him as if he understands. And I for one want to thank him for the errors and beauty he's drawn to our attention today. This undue buoyancy of his . . . well, I count myself lucky if my strength proves equal to the task of looking the bastard in the eye. Step away from that jangling marionette, ladies and gentlemen – yes, damn the attackers for their importance and officers. Maquette's the name, eh? Well, as a citizen of Accomplice she has the same rights given all of us.'

'Which are?' someone said.

'And tomorrow, in a special ceremony in the town square, I shall present her with the key to the city. After all, if you prick her, does she not bleed?'

'Frankly, no.'

Rudloe, aware of gathering press photographers, ignored the argument. His face was set in such a strain of stern resolve that his lower jaw, jutting out beyond the upper, fractured across the middle.

When the red myrmidon returned empty-handed, the Grand Dollimo smiled sadly, unsurprised. He ordered Distaff Plastique to lay on the desk and activated the cabinet gears – the sentry lowered out of sight, the desktop closing over it.

The obfuscations of priestcraft got uglier every year, thought the Dollimo. He pressured the wall at the right spot to open the layered door marked NO ENTRY. Passing through, he waited for the door to close behind him and removed his bowler, glass mask and gloves, tossing them onto an ornate rosewood side-table.

Nowhere to be seen was the huge android scorpion bed of lore. No mechanical crucifix deployed its legs on the wall. In fact he hated a successful equation the way he hated a cheap frame – it wasn't worthy of what it was meant to bear.

The room was one of snug and opulent domesticity, all warm lamps and rich velvet. The Dollimo kicked off his shoes, pulled on his slippers and walked across a thick red carpet to the drinks cabinet, pouring himself a sherry. Then he sat into the deeps of an armchair, lit a pipe, and opened the newspaper.

Barny, Edgy and Gregor attended the wedding of Dietrich and Gettysburg the following day. Maquette handed over the ring, actually a funny antique fuse like a cork wire, which she had found on the back of her head. As a sea captain EH Hunt had full powers to wed and was chuffed that someone finally acknowledged the truth of his assertions. The two demons, one in battered armour and one in white leather, stood before the main observatory window as applause and confetti rained upon them and beer and wolf tart were served. Edgy talked about his profits from selling the harpy meat, not enough to open the bar. Half of it would be lost on medical bills due to his being beaten up by those who had found their pies filled with everyday lard. Gregor, too, had a smashed nose, but without the threat of legal action hanging over his head, he could think clearly. He was trying to develop a line of rigid front-buttoning balaclavas called 'head jackets' and couldn't stop laughing. Barny, fully visible again, stood sad amid the festivities with a chimp on his shoulder as Maquette rode Mister Braintree around the place. BB Henrietta was feeding wolf tart to the blind astronomer despite the fact that he was trying to give a speech.

'We mix and effect. Shirts beloved, make the water change. When young I was an iconoclast, ignoring gulls until they left and weeping unusually fast to get it over with. And I thought, "One day my own fault will be enough". Today I turn sideways, try to force arms and nose into an envelope. A lot of things are possible, I'll tell you, but a simple thing like that? Not in this basket of bloody tempers.' He wrenched impotently at his wicker chair. 'But ideas endure in the whirlwind. My age allows me a certain latitude. I give you a puzzle desk full of snakes. I give you the red velvet which lines the inside of my skull. I flash last week at you as though it were ancient and valuable knowledge. The following is on me. Police – mental bowels. Pedestrian – unpaid clown. Life plan – a safe full of autumn leaves. Never belong to your work. Sorrow hangs our arms at our sides and pays no money. Passion is ridiculous only in fishes. A man should kick with the bright side of his trousers. Death is a little minute of white like a full stop. In the buzzing cream of the summer air, we prepare to be angels, the world prepares to be left behind by us all. Out there, I can feel the picture completing itself. A thick-backed man walks the streets away from hope, the colour of striped noise approaches Accomplice, the great bug prepares to shed itself, and the settling earth fills a thousand dead mouths all the deeper. To the happy couple.'

Barny looked thoughtful as the toast was given.

Dietrich leaned to Gettysburg. 'You liked to say that fools cast an honest shadow. I've realised everyone does.'

*

Later that day, the Mayor stood on the palace balcony with a brace across his lower jaw and, pausing to state something about 'postponing my bloody overthrow' to the assembled masses, presented Maquette with the key to the city. He looked ahead with a rigid expression as she inserted it into her heart and cranked it like a starting handle.